SEASON OF MEMORIES

MURPHY BROTHER STORIES, BOOK 9

JENNIFER RODEWALD

Rooted Publishing

ROOTED PUBLISHING

Season of Memories

ISBN: 979-8-9874510-0-7

Any references to events, real people, or real places are used fictitiously. Names, characters, and places are products of the author's imagination, and any similarities to real events are purely accidental.

Front-cover image from shutterstock.com and purchased for licenced use. Design by Jennifer Rodewald.

First printing edition 2022.

Rooted Publishing

McCook, NE 69001

Email: jen@authorjenrodewald.com

https://authorjenrodewald.com/

Scripture quotations taken from the Holy Bible, New International Version®, NIV®. Copyright ©1973, 1978, 1984, 2011 by Biblica, Inc. Used by permission of Zondervan. All rights reserved worldwide. www.zondervan.com The "NIV" and "New International Version" are trademarks registered in the United States Patent and Trademark Office by Biblica, Inc.

Scriptures quotations taken from the NKJV are taken from the NEW KING JAMES VERSION (NKJV): Scripture taken from the NEW KING JAMES VERSION®. Copyright© 1982 by Thomas Nelson, Inc. Used by permission. All rights reserved.

CONTENTS

We will not hide them from their children,
Telling to the generation to come the praises of the Lord,
And His strength and His wonderful works that He has done.
Psalm 78:4

For my grandparents,
most of whom are rejoicing with their Savior.
Your lives shifted our family trajectory,
and you have given me a beautiful legacy.
I am grateful.

CHAPTER ONE

(in which God is good)

"**D**ad? Are you hearing me?"

Tyler's voice seemed to come from a hollow distance. With one palm braced against a two-by-four stud, Kevin Murphy inhaled deeply, but he kept the breath controlled and subtle. *No need to panic.* The wave of painful pressure in the middle of his chest subsided. He curled his fingers into the wood, his hand trembling. *Indigestion. Just an excess of jalapenos on my street tacos . . .*

Wiping the perspiration from his forehead, Kevin swallowed and looked at his son. "I'm sorry, Ty. Say that again, will you?"

Tyler's eyes pinched with mild concern as he lowered the speed square in his hand until it rested against his good leg. For a beat, he studied Kevin. "I met Jade when Connor brought her to Matt's before Thanksgiving. You'll like her, I promise."

Seemed off that Ty felt he needed to convince Kevin of Jade's virtues. If Connor was interested in this woman who had moved into the cabin next to his, then Kevin should trust his son's judgment. Connor was the steady-on sort. He'd rarely been led off track. Not to mention, he was a full-grown, life-tested man. One who deserved to know the sweet joy of the happiness found in love again.

Should trust.

Trusting Connor's judgment wasn't the issue. The real problem was this fatherly surge of protectiveness that, even after well past thirty years of parenting, pulsed strong and unyielding. Losing Sadie had devastated his son, and Kevin had barely borne the pain of watching one of his boys go through that kind of anguish. A father shouldn't have to witness that sort of loss for his children—it was a unique agony that Kevin had yet to fully work through.

The last thing Connor needed was more heartache. And if Kevin knew anything was certain in life, it was that relationships always came with heartaches.

They bring blessings too!

Yes. There was that, and Kevin was fighting hard to keep that at the forefront of his mind when he thought about Connor and this new woman. The thought kept colliding with the counterargument that a divorced woman with two kids would bring in a whole lot of complications—a fact that was bound to add a bonus level of heartache.

But God works in hard places!

An undefined thread of something strong and *not* good ribboned around Kevin's gut, as it had more than a few times when he'd thought on his third-born son these days. Undefined only because Kevin had flat out refused to name it. And the emotion wasn't directed at his son.

Distrust. Resentment. Anger. Any of those labels would likely fit . . . If only he'd be honest.

A fresh squeeze gripped Kevin's chest before that thought could fully land. This time there was no hiding the wrenching pain that stole his breath, wringing out a hard grunt as he sagged against the framing at his side.

"Dad?" Ty dropped the speed square and pivoted on his prosthetic leg before he hobble-leaped toward Kevin.

"I'm—" Kevin held out a hand, but he couldn't finish the claim that he was fine. The world blurred out of focus, becoming a hazy mess of two-by-fours and power tools. Then Ty's dark eyes filled his view with wide panic. Swallowing, Kevin moved his lips again, intending to say he was fine.

He *needed* to be fine. There were things left unreconciled between him and this life—his heart and God's.

Instead, the increasingly cruel vise gripping within forced a groan from deep in his chest.

"Dad!" Ty's iron grip clamped on Kevin's shoulder, preventing his collapse to the ground.

Strange. Sweat seeped from Kevin's pores, but he felt so chilled that his son's meaty hand almost burned against his skin.

A dark fog invaded the blur that had been Kevin's vision, and the sound of spring-melt powered waters filled his ears. This was not the work of jalapenos. This was much more serious.

"Heart att—" Had he mumbled that?

"Hang on, Dad." Tyler's voice rumbled above him. Seemed like it came from a long distance. And why from above? He and Ty were nearly the same height.

"Ambulance is on its way . . ."

It'd been a very long time since he'd ridden in an ambulance. Since Connor had been a swell in Helen's belly. That had been the turning point. The catalyst.

Beauty from ashes . . .

"Hang on, Dad."

Emotion cracked in his son's voice, pulling an ache from Kevin's soul. Ty had already lost so much in life, and his fall into darkness had been nearly as severe as Kevin's had once been. He hadn't wanted any of his boys to stumble down the path of addiction that he'd trod. Had prayed from the moment he'd truly become a praying man that they wouldn't. Watching Ty do so had been excruciating.

Please, God, don't let him go down that road again . . .

"Just, hang on. I'll tell Mom to meet us . . ."

Helen. His beloved. Her darling image drifted into his mind, easing the pain seizing his heart. She was his sunshine. His favorite.

He'd come so very close to destroying her. Truth be told, he *had* wrecked her. He'd wrecked them. There was no earthly reason that Kevin, let alone his marriage, should have survived those years. He shouldn't have even made it into that ambulance alive.

It had been a miracle. Two miracles wrapped up in one. A second chance at life and love—one he hadn't deserved.

Remember grace . . .

The scream of sirens broke through Kevin's dimming consciousness, a faded, surreal sound that came from the distant past as much as it did from that moment.

"God, please . . ." Tears salted Ty's whispered prayer.

Kevin forced his mind to focus on reaching for his boy. He gripped the neck of the man who held him against his burly chest. The man who had once been his little boy, a baby he could remember holding because he'd been sober by then.

"Ty."

"Yeah, Dad. I've got you. Stay with me, okay?"

Another groan escaped as Kevin exhaled through the pain. He didn't want to die like this—with his son holding on to him. It would rock his core. Ty had already passed through a fire, walking through a story Kevin hadn't wanted for him.

He hadn't wanted any of the hard things his boys had journeyed through.

Even so. *Remember . . .*

There had been grace. Great grace. The sort of grace that had reached a drunken young man who was destroying his life and his young family. The kind of grace that changed a life.

His life.

That undefined thread of something strong and *not* good loosened its noose. Kevin exhaled a ragged breath. It was long overdue—this releasing.

The Lord is gracious and compassionate, slow to anger and abounding in good.

Still true. Though they'd passed through rough waters—several times over, *He* had been there. Every time.

Bless the Lord, oh my soul, and all that is within me, bless His holy name.

He hadn't been doing so well on that one lately. Not truly, in the depths of his heart. But if this was to be his dying day . . .

Kevin moved his hand until he cupped the back of Tyler's head. His son folded until his forehead pressed against Kevin's.

"Dad . . ."

"God is good." Kevin breathed out those last three words before the inky blackness claimed him.

With her left hand, Helen Murphy scrolled through the Pinterest board she'd labeled *homecoming*, a pen poised at the ready in her right. They would all be there this year. In just a couple of weeks, she'd have all seven boys and their families for Christmas.

She nearly burst with joy.

Seven boys, now men. Six daughters-in-love and one who would likely become so very soon, if Lauren's instincts were correct. How lovely, that. They would always miss Sadie. Forever. But Connor didn't need to live out the rest of his days alone—Sadie wouldn't have wanted that for him or for her son, Reid. And Lauren, Matt's wife, seemed to adore Jade Beck.

So. Seven boys and their plus-ones. Fourteen. Now, for the grands.

A giddiness bubbled up from Helen's soul. Was there any comparable delight to one's grandchildren? Nope. Not that Helen knew of.

She'd have sugar cookies and royal icing ready. And sprinkles! Gads of them. Oh, they'd make such a glorious mess! And *eat*. Yes sir, they would eat. All the sugar they wanted, because they'd be at their gran's house! It would be fabulous fun. Helen tapped her feet against the wood floor in anticipation.

Now then, for the count. Matt's three. Jacob's two. Between Connor and Jade there were three—and she couldn't wait to meet one Miss Lily Beck and young Mr. Kellen. Over text, Reid had promised that she would like them both. So that put her up to eight.

Jackson was up to four, because that son was always in it to win it, no matter what *it* was. That made twelve.

Ty had sweet little Ella and Evan and a baby boy due in February. Helen supposed she shouldn't count the one in the oven for this purpose. No bed or place setting needed yet.

Fourteen.

As yet, no littles for Brandon and Megan.

And that brought her to Brayden, the son who'd landed the farthest from home. Goodness, but she missed them. But they were coming, bringing little Isaac with them, and hallelujah for it!

"Fifteen grands and more on the way!" Helen dropped her pen, clapped her hands with delight, and then lifted them above her head, palms up. "Lord, you have been good!"

Seven boys to fifteen grands. Not a bad return on investment. Helen giggled as she stood and tapped out a happy dance on her way to the kitchen.

She was ridiculous. She knew it. But who could blame her? Besides, one *should* delight—ridiculously so—in the goodness of God.

The phone she'd left on the table chimed for an incoming call as she filled her water glass. Still grinning, she took a sip and sashayed over to the great wooden gathering point that Kevin had built for her. Goodness, that man. If she'd dreamed up a tower ten stories tall and carved with pomegranates, he'd build it for her.

Her glance shifted toward the thick wooden beam in her sunroom. The one Kevin had carved *Kevin loves Helen* inside a heart at completion of that project—another one of her ideas.

Love swelled into that bursting of joy already in her heart.

For better or worse . . .

They'd seen worse. They'd known darkness and storms and nights laden with shouts and tears and even hopelessness. It had seemed for a time that they wouldn't make it. But even then, in that darkest season of her life, she'd known Kevin had loved her. Not well at that moment, but he did love her, and she'd loved him.

And then it got better. By the mighty grace of God, their marriage was reborn.

But Helen didn't have time to dwell on those memories. She reached for the phone on the table, noting Ty's name on the screen.

With a smile, she answered. "Hi, son. How's the build going?"

"Mom."

One word. One breath. That was all it took to send her heart plummeting to the floor.

"What's wrong, Ty?"

"Dad . . ." The deep voice on the other side of the call cracked, and Ty cleared his throat. "Dad is having a heart attack."

"What?" Helen's knees buckled, and she landed on the chair she'd thankfully left pulled out. "He was fine this morning . . ."

"We're en route to the hospital. Should be there in fifteen minutes."

"Are you with him?"

"Following the ambulance."

The trembling started in her core and worked its way out to her limbs, strengthening as the moments passed.

"Mom, can you get yourself there? I can call Jacob—"

"I'm leaving now." She was up and halfway to the door.

She hung up, not knowing if Ty had said goodbye or not. Didn't matter. All she could think about was getting to the hospital. Getting to Kevin.

"God . . ." Her voice quavered on the whispered prayer. That was it, all she had.

A heart attack. The love of her life was in an ambulance with a heart attack. Her heart was already breaking.

CHAPTER TWO

(in which time becomes confused)

V oices drifted around him. They seemed clipped and urgent and another world away. He had no idea what was being said or why there seemed to be this scurry of chaos orbiting him.

Kevin pressed his head back and exhaled through a vice-clamped chest. A deep, guttural moan filled his hearing. Did that come from his throat? It sounded painful and perhaps desperate.

Stay with us, Mr. Murphy . . .

Something warm and numbing slogged through his veins, claiming his already foggy mind. Had he been drinking?

Hadn't he quit drinking?

He had. Because drinking had very nearly ruined his life. Surely his sobriety was real . . .

Keep fighting, sir. Stay with us . . .

In the murkiness of that moment, with his mind blurry and reality smudged, Kevin wasn't sure. This moment seemed so disappointingly familiar, as if he'd lived this once before.

Because he had, hadn't he?

God, I don't want to be that man anymore. Please . . .

The thought seemed as much a memory as it was a prayer. Time became a blotchy mess—the past confused with the present. Kevin couldn't sort out history from present reality.

And then with sudden breathtaking clarity, he was in 1982. Living a moment that felt more real and current than the fading confusion of stern voices and something beeping incessantly.

Man, it was hot. So, so hot, especially for December.

Twenty-year-old Kevin Murphy shook out his arms and peeked around the wall separating the hallway from that dim sanctuary. Candlelight flickered from the cluster of taper candles in the gaudy holders on each side of the aisle. Maybe that was why it was so hot? There sure were a lot of those flickering little flames. Seemed they'd like to lick his soul.

Why did church always make him feel like he was in hell? No one even had to breathe a brimstone-filled word, and he still felt the scorch of eternal flames coming for him.

Imagine that for all eternity.

He didn't want to. More, he wouldn't. Specifically, not on that day.

Kevin tugged on the sleeves of his rented black tux and drew in a long, fortifying breath. Jim Beam tinged the air he released, summoning a strong need for another nip. Turning to the guy at his right and slightly behind him, he tapped his best man's chest and motioned with his fingers. "I need a drink."

"We're in *church*, and it's just about time, Kev," Dave said. "Think you've had enough."

Kevin wiggled his fingers again. "One more, for luck."

"Second thoughts?" Dave's expression furrowed. "It's not too—"

With a scowl, Kevin slipped his hand into Dave's suit jacket, fishing the inner breast pocket for the flask he'd entrusted to Dave before they'd left the trailer. Jackpot.

"No." He untwisted the small cap, tipped back a long swig, and replaced the lid. "It's just hot in here."

Dave lifted one skeptical brow. "It's Christmas Eve. And snowing. And the heater's not working great in here. Maybe you're not ready—"

"Shut up, Dave." Kevin gave his best man a healthy shove. "Just wait until it's you."

"It'll be a while." Dave shouldered him back, then adjusted his bowtie. "But if it were me and I loved the girl, I wouldn't need liquid fire to get me through my own wedding."

Trust him for that. Dave, upstanding as the mountain winters were long, would never be caught up in the vices that Kevin had been born to. Then again, why would he? Raised by a pair of do-good Christian parents whose most serious reoccurring problem was getting to Sunday services on time, Dave always had plenty at the table and never had to wonder how he'd make it to school if his dad's binge had him strung out until late in the day. He never knew what it was like to bear the label of the town-drunk's kid. Dave walked through life like it was all sunshine and happiness.

And Kevin was truly glad for him. He didn't wish his own life on his best friend.

All that being so, Dave wasn't right about the current state of difficulties. Loving the girl wasn't the problem. Kevin loved Helen. One hundred percent, all his heart loved her. Had since the day he met her when she was working at the Ice Cream Palooza the summer before. Her blue eyes had connected with his gaze, and in the space of three heartbeats he knew he had to make that pretty blonde with the shy smile his.

Lucky for him, Helen had felt the same. For Kevin and Helen-almost-Murphy, love at first sight was as real as the church he was standing in.

No sir, loving Helen was not the issue. The problem was that life looked a little big, standing there in that dark hallway, waiting to promise to take responsibility for a family.

Anxiety wound through his gut and pulled tight. *Family.* No one knew—just Helen and him. Probably they suspected. After all, this wedding was tossed together in a hurry. But he hadn't told anyone—not even his lifelong best buddy Dave. And Helen had promised she wouldn't say anything. She'd simply meet him in between those fancy candelabras at the front of the church, wearing a white dress, and they'd make it all right.

It *was* going to be all right. It was going to be great. He could be a husband. A dad. Even if he didn't know what that looked like, given the louse of a father he'd grown up with. He'd figure it out and sure as anything do better than his dad had ever done.

He most certainly couldn't do worse.

The cord around his chest pulled harder, and Kevin moved to fish out that flask again.

"Not this time." Dave intercepted his trespassing hand. "Music is changing." With a firm grip on Kevin's shoulders, Dave turned him toward the sanctuary. When Kevin thought he'd be pushed forward, Dave leaned over his shoulder instead. "Helen's a catch. And she loves you. Do right by her, Kev."

Before Kevin could turn a glare on his overbearing friend, he was nudged forward. Numbly—partially due to Jimmy Beam's intervention, thank you very much—Kevin found his place near the pastor he'd met only the day before at the rehearsal. The man shot him a wide smile and flashed a thumbs-up near his hip.

Gripping one hand with the other, Kevin turned to watch the sauntering up the aisle. First, two bridesmaids. Helen's best girlfriends from high school. They looked better suited to a cheerleading outfit than to preceding their friend down the bridal way.

Man, they were *really* young.

He wasn't even old enough to legally buy the stuff he'd been sucking down all morning. Helen was only eighteen. Could they really be ready for marriage, let alone a kid?

He needed another drink. Too bad that was entirely out of the question, Dave being the inconveniently resolute type. And the both of them standing out there in front of everyone.

The music changed again, and the small gathering of witnesses stood. Kevin shifted his gaze from the flower girl, who had just littered the runway with fake red rose petals. A puff of white flounced near the doors opposite, the shadows cloaking the woman lost within the masses of poofy sleeves and frilly white lace. More, the white hat, anchored at an angle on her blonde hair, blocked her face from him as she looked down. Her face remained tilted floorward as she floated toward him. Hopefully, because she had to watch her step. Not because she couldn't look at him.

But he needed, desperately, for her to look at him. Because this rising urge to bolt was becoming harder and harder to control.

Look at me. Tell me you love me. You'll stay with me . . .

Just when he thought he couldn't stay rooted, her blue eyes lifted, connecting with his searching gaze.

Kevin's lips parted as his breath caught. *Helen*, he mouthed.

She gave him a closed-lip smile. Well, smile was a little generous. Grin? Not that either.

She was scared too. But there she was, now before him. Ready to take his hand, his name.

With eyes wide and glazed with unshed tears, Helen held his stare as her father transferred her hand to Kevin's. After a long-held and suspiciously disapproving look, her dad proclaimed that "her mother and I" gave Helen to be Kevin's wife. And then it was just Helen and him standing before God and man to pledge their lives to each other.

"You came," she whispered, a mix of relief and nerves in her voice.

Kevin tucked her hand into the crook of his arm and leaned down to whisper, "I said I would."

Her nose wrinkled, and she drew back the slightest bit. By her mild scowl, she could smell the bourbon on his breath. Her lips flattened, and she swallowed.

"Last time," Kevin said as together they stepped toward the grinning pastor. "Promise."

Helen didn't look at him as she blinked rapidly.

He knew why. She'd heard that before.

In his defense, though, he wasn't actually drunk. So the last time he promised her that it would be the last time was still the truth.

Even so, Helen's pinched expression told him exactly what she thought—even if she tried to hide it behind a tight smile as she stared forward.

Look at me. Tell me you love me. You'll stay with me . . .

She did look up at him again, turning her body to face him as the grinning fool before them had instructed. Those blue eyes softened as he stared down at her. Even so, within those beautiful depths, beneath the love she gave him so freely, there was reserve. Perhaps fear.

Maybe neither of them was really ready for this . . .

Here was the thing though. She was everything good in his world—a world that had been filled with gray loneliness most of his life. He needed her. He loved her. And just like Dave had charged him to do so, he would do right by her.

He promised her right there, in his heart. He would.

Helen stared out the window overlooking the hospital grounds, her nails biting into her palms as she watched snow drift toward the ground. Two hours before, she was all giddy joy, planning Christmas with the grandchildren. Now she barely held back tears.

"Mom." Tyler stood beside her, his large, rough hand cupping her elbow. "Why don't you sit?"

She continued to watch the snow. It was so gentle. Beautiful.

"I can't," she breathed. If she moved away, looked from the mesmerizing beauty, she'd have to face her sons. Jacob had arrived moments after she'd stepped through the ER doors. Ty insisted he wasn't leaving, even though his drive home would be more than an hour long and over a snowy pass.

They wanted to be there. For her. And the father they looked up to. They wanted to lend her strength and courage. Thing was, if she turned to face them, she'd fall to pieces. She knew she would.

Merely the thought of it rocked emotion from the depths of her soul. Hugging herself with one arm, she grasped the pendent of blue topaz that she'd worn for nearly thirty-six years. A gift from her beloved for their fourth anniversary. A splurge that they couldn't afford back then, but it'd meant the world to her—to them both. Because they were still married at that point, and the year before it had looked very much like they wouldn't make it that far. There had been moments, in fact, when it hadn't looked like Kevin would make it at all.

That had been *after*.

After Kevin had nearly taken his life driving drunk, landing himself here. In that very hospital, thirty-seven years before.

Helen shut her eyes as that awful season of her life replayed.

It had been a couple of days since she'd heard from him. Tears had filled the hours when the boys were sleeping or were sufficiently distracted by Mr. Rogers or *Sesame Street*. She'd tried to hide them from her toddlers. But as she made a lunch of boxed macaroni and cheese and orange slices, Helen couldn't keep the streams from flowing.

"Daddy home tonight?" Matt had asked ten minutes before.

Swallowing the hard lump in her throat, Helen had forced a tight smile at her oldest son. "I don't think so, Matty."

"He still workin'." Matt nodded his head, all proud and firm. Certain his dad was out there doing good things to take care of this rapidly growing family.

Helen wrapped his little three-year-old body with one arm and squeezed. Rather than answering him—because how long was she going to keep up this lie?—she simply kissed his dark hair and carried him over to their small secondhand loveseat. "You and Jacob watch Big Bird while I get your lunch ready. Tina is coming over to play with you tonight."

From his seat on the sofa, Matt scrunched his nose at her. "You gone again?"

Ache squeezed Helen's heart as she replayed the disappointment in her oldest boy's expression. She didn't want to be gone from them in the evenings. Didn't want to miss bedtime stories and good-night kisses. But even a dingy trailer cost money. Not to mention having babies.

That ache hadn't eased in the minutes that it'd taken to get the boys settled in front of the TV and then start the mac 'n' cheese. Lowering the wooden spoon she'd been stirring the pasta with, Helen covered the small bump of her womb. Three babies in less than four years. Eye-yah. She and Kevin were not doing well on a lot of things, but apparently making babies was not a weakness with them.

With a glance over her shoulder, she peeked at the boys. They sat together, Matty's arm draped over baby Jacob's shoulders. One with dark hair who looked an awful lot like his way-more-hand-some-than-was-good-for-him father. The other fairer, with blue eyes—the son who looked like her. Seemed like that should have been a good place to stop—one boy looking like dad and one looking like mom. Sufficiently blessed. Especially considering their finances.

More especially, considering Kevin's rapidly increasing drinking habit.

"His dad is a drunk, Helen."

"Oh, Daddy. Kevin isn't his father."

"No?" Daddy crossed his arms. "Why did I find a fleet of empty beer bottles in the back of that ugly wreck of a truck he drives?"

One of several discussions she'd had with her father about the boy she had been dating the summer after her senior year. They'd always ended the same way: Daddy telling her to be careful and not to make choices she'd end up regretting. She promising him and then begging him, with everything sweet and hopeful in her, to please just give Kevin a chance.

That was all Kevin needed—a chance. She'd been certain of it. He was thoughtful and kind. He knew how to work hard. And he didn't like his dad—didn't want to be anything like him.

He needed a chance to be something more than the town-drunk's son.

Three and a half years into a headlong marriage because of a night gone too far in the back of that wreck of a truck, and Helen wasn't so sure.

Heaven help her though, she did love him. Even with the steep plunge into crushing disappointment. Even with the way he was breaking her heart.

Tell me you love me, Helen. Kevin's pleas, spoken over the phone the morning after she'd told him he couldn't come home drunk—not again—echoed with crystal clarity in her mind. *Say you'll stay with me.*

He had slayed her with that. Every. Time. Because she knew that Kevin meant those words with his whole damaged heart. The issue had never been that she thought he didn't love her. He did.

He just loved a bottle as much. Sometimes more. Or perhaps his father had handed him a legacy Kevin could not break away from no matter how much he resented it. Helen wasn't sure which.

The first year she'd let Kevin's drinking go without much more than a mild complaint. After all, he wasn't a loud drunk. Wasn't violent. Usually he just came home and passed out. Or was delivered home by Dave. But the thing was, alcohol was expensive. And the other more important thing was, she'd seen how his father had turned out. Had held Kevin's stiff hand when they'd buried his dead-beat dad after a binge gone wrong shortly after Jacob had been born.

As much as Kevin disliked the man who had raised him in a nearly-always-drunk fog, her husband was barreling toward that same end.

Helen didn't want that for him. And she didn't want that for her boys. Deep down she *knew* Kevin didn't want it either.

So she started making herself a little louder. Her protests a little firmer.

Rather than seeing what she saw and working on the problem, Kevin pulled away. Went out more frequently. Sank deeper into this alcoholic abyss.

Three days ago Helen had finally stood her ground.

He'd called to tell her he'd be late—was going out with the boys after his shift at the sawmill.

"You can't come home drunk," she'd told him.

"What?" His response sounded more caught off guard than anything.

"You can't keep doing this, Kevin. The boys are watching."

"I never do anything *really* bad."

"You have sons who look up to you. Sons who, right now, want to be just like you. Know what Matt said yesterday? He said, 'Daddy is all wobbly and silly at night.'" She cringed at the memory of Matt mimicking his wobbly and silly father. Whatever Kevin's father had handed to Kevin, this was not the legacy she wanted for her kids. "How long do you think it'll take him to realize why that really is?"

"He's only two."

"Matt is three, going on four." What dad didn't know his own kid's age? *The one who spent most of that baby's life drunk.* Helen grew more resolute. "Is this the dad you want to be, Kevin?"

A long, telling silence followed. Then with a tight voice, Kevin barked at her. "Look. They'll be in bed by the time I get home anyway."

"You can't come home drunk."

"It's my house!" Now he was angry.

"It's mine too, and we are barely making rent payments. One day it might be you drink too much of your paycheck away and we get kicked out. Then what?"

"I wouldn't do that." Kevin became all soft assurance.

A tear had trickled onto her cheek, because he'd said something like that to her before they were married. Only in that conversation, she'd told him she was a little afraid to be with him because of his dad. *I'm not gonna be like him, baby. I wouldn't do that to you.*

It was turning out that her Daddy had been right.

"You promised me, Kevin." She sniffed and then swallowed the rest of her cry. She wasn't going to be weak on this. "Do you remember that?"

Another long pause. Then, "Helen . . ."

"I mean it, Kevin. My dad came over and changed the locks. If you're not home by dark, and sober, you're not coming in."

"What!" All reasonable gentleness left his voice.

Helen drew in a fortifying breath, then plunged in deeper. "This is the way it's going to be. We have two boys and another baby on the way. It's time to stop this. I'm not going to sit here doing nothing while you drink your way into becoming just like your dad. I won't do it, Kevin."

An angry string of ugly words Helen would never let pass her own lips came from the man she loved. At the end of that tirade, he said, "I'm going out tonight with the guys. That's the end of it."

"Then you've made your choice." She hung up before he could respond. Four hours later, the phone in the kitchen rang again. This time, it was Dave. "Hi, Helen."

"Is he drunk?"

"You know the answer."

"Then don't bring him here."

"Yeah, I heard about your conversation. He's spent the night swinging back and forth between boiling mad and desperately hoping you'll stay with him." Dave cleared his throat. "Stand your ground. I've got you on this, Helen. I just wanted you to know I'm taking him to his dad's. He's fine. I'm sure he'll sleep it off and call you tomorrow."

"Okay."

"Helen?"

"Yeah."

"I mean it. Stay strong. Like I said, I'm with you. Whatever you need—you or the boys—just let me know."

"I need a miracle, Dave." Bitterness seeped through her heart and salted her voice. "You have one of those?"

"Not in my back pocket, no. But I know a Guy." His attempt at humor fell flat. Again, Dave cleared his throat. "Seriously, though, Helen. I'm praying for you both. You do know that, right?"

Helen didn't know how to respond to that. She wanted to spit out a *pray harder because it's not working*, but Dave was a good friend. Had been to Kevin his whole life and to her since the day she and Kevin met. He didn't deserve her bitter sarcasm.

The following morning, Helen received a phone call from a repentant husband. He seemed repentant at first anyway.

"That was the last time, baby. I promise."

Promises made and broken many times before. Helen remained quiet.

"Tell me you love me, Helen. Say you'll stay with me."

"I do love you, Kevin. And I'm not going anywhere." She sighed, lowering herself onto a chair beside the phone, speaking softly so the boys, who were playing dinosaurs across the room, couldn't hear her. "But you can't come here—not drunk. Not anymore."

"Why are you kicking me out of my own home?"

She didn't want to fight him—wasn't sure she'd have the strength to stay the course. She was bone tired. Pregnant, two toddlers, a husband with a drinking problem, and as of the week before, working at the truck-stop diner three evenings a week. How long could she hold up?

Despite her efforts to hold back the tears, a few dripped onto her nose, and she turned to face the window so the boys wouldn't see. "I'm not." Her voice cracked. "Oh, Kevin, how could you put me in this position? I love you. The boys and I need you. But you can't keep doing this. You can't become your father."

"I am *not* my dad." Leaded anger weighed his voice.

Helen didn't respond. For several heart-throbbing breaths, there was silence on the line. And then . . . then a hard click.

He'd hung up on her. That had been the last time she'd talk to him.

Shoulders hunched, Helen leaned against the side of the refrigerator. In the background, Sally Ride was counting backward from ten for Grundgetta's garbage can launch on *Sesame Street*. The boys remained transfixed on the screen. And Helen—

Helen caved to the quivering sobs that surged up. Hands covering her face, she muffled her cries as best that she could.

"God," she whispered. "If you're listening, if you can see me . . ."

Dave's mom promised that God could. Several times over Mrs. Clayton had assured Helen during one of their weekly coffee get-togethers that God saw her. That God cared about her.

But . . . but I'm not a good enough person, Helen had argued. *I got pregnant, and I lied to my parents, and now I have these beautiful boys and Kevin and me are only going to wreck them. Maybe this is God's punishment to me for—*

Mrs. Clayton had cut her off right there. *Your children are a gift, Helen. Don't ever mistake that. Those boys are a gift from God, not a punishment.* And she'd opened her Bible to show her that it really did say that in there.

Children are a heritage from the Lord.

Over the past several months, Mrs. Clayton had shown Helen other verses in the Bible too. Things like *All have sinned and fallen short of the glory of God.* And *God demonstrates His love toward us in this: that while we were still sinners, Christ died for us.* And the most befuddling one, simple as the words may be, *Believe on the Lord Jesus Christ and you will be saved.*

Saved to an eternity of life with God in heaven.

Mrs. Clayton had been firm in that claim every time Helen had hinted that God wasn't interested in her because she wasn't good enough.

No one is good enough. We all need saved.

It all was confusing to Helen. And seemed a little bit irrelevant. Because while eternity might be a long time—as in forever—what Helen felt she needed right then was a God who would shake the alcoholism out of her husband right there on earth. And soon. She needed a God who would give Kevin the willpower to be the man he wanted to be.

She needed a God who would see her sorry state of life right then and there and intervene.

Helen tipped her head back and swiped the tears from her face. As she stared at the water-stained ceiling tiles, a surge of anger pushed up from her soul. "Are you that God?"

No whispers from heaven came forth. No touch from an angel or a phone call from the man saying a miracle had just happened. The splash-hiss sound of water boiling over onto the electric coils of the stove was her only answer. Helen jerked herself off the refrigerator and moved to rescue the pasta sure to be burning at the bottom of the pan.

She'd never felt so alone and miserable in her life. And felt no hope for change.

CHAPTER THREE

(in which prayers can be hard)

"Mom."

A pair of large, work-strengthened hands warmed her shoulders and squeezed.

Shutting her eyes, her heart throbbing with an ache that had a significant portion in the recall of the past, Helen drew in a long breath before she turned to face Tyler.

Sometimes hard things must be remembered. Not dwelled on. Not invited to hijack the present or the future. But still, they should be recalled on occasion. Because if that time hadn't been so hard, perhaps the grace that had poured out wouldn't be quite so amazing.

She and Kevin had experienced amazing grace. And this young man behind her, now a husband and father himself, was one of so many proofs.

Yahweh, the lord of heaven *and* earth, was indeed that God she'd needed. The One who could and did intervene in her life and in Kevin's. And the One who now and forevermore held them both securely in his hands. No matter how this day turned out.

Tyler's hands rubbed her arms, and Helen looked up.

"Matt is coming."

Helen shook her head. "He shouldn't. Not now—it's nearly dark, and there's snow on the pass."

"Lauren insisted he come." Tyler's expression became resolved—a look he'd inherited from Kevin on the occasions that stern determination was needed.

Jacob joined his younger but bigger brother, and together the pair made a protective little cove around her. "Connor said he'll come this way in the morning but to keep him updated. Brandon too. Brayden is flying in tomorrow afternoon. Jackson will wait until he lands, and then they'll both head up the hills this way."

A lump swelled in Helen's throat. "It's too soon to make these plans. We don't know what will happen."

Tyler shook his head, compassion and worry saturating his dark eyes. "Dad was always there for us. Always."

Jacob nodded solemnly. "And you—we'll be here for you both, no matter what comes." Her fair son—the only one of the seven who looked like her—draped an arm around her frame. A move that held such significance to Helen's heart, as only a few years back, Jacob had been aloof and taciturn. Their years-long conflict and his seeming rejection of not just her but of their whole family had been such a painful season.

Thank God for reconciliation.

Helen pressed her head into his shoulder.

"Don't worry about the house or anything like that, okay, Mom?" Jacob pulled her in tighter. "Kate is going over right after she gets the kids fed. She'll make sure the rooms are all in order, and she'll see that the cabin and Gert are ready for people as well."

That pricked a small smile and sparked a touch of laughter in her heart, a thing that seemed so monumental considering their situation. When Kate had become Helen's first daughter-in-law, no one would have thought that she would even know how to prep bedrooms for people, let alone a skoolie. But years had a way of changing people—sometimes for the worst and sometimes for the better. Helen was convinced that her people had grown for the better.

Helen found Jacob's blue eyes. "Maybe it's about time your dad and I try that boondocking life."

The man grinned and nodded. "You'd like it. Gertrude is the best little house on wheels you could ask for, and Kate and I can give you all the best pointers."

They had talked about it, she and Kevin. Often. Had even purchased Gertrude the Skoolie from Jacob and Kate several years back. Kevin just needed to figure out how to slow down a bit. How to hand over the reins to his construction business completely into Tyler's capable hands. And specifically over the past two years, how to lay down the things that plagued his heart. The disappointments that had hit him harder than he'd been prepared for and had put him into an exhausting wrestling match with God.

It just doesn't seem fair, Helen. Watching Connor go through this when we'd all believed. When he's worked his whole life to do what is right and good . . . I know that it's small and weak of me, but I can't get past it . . .

Helen had cried with her husband many times, many nights. Because, though she didn't battle the resentment the same way Kevin did, she knew what he meant. Watching your son lose the love of his life wasn't something any parent ever wanted to experience. And while Kevin feared that Helen would think less of him by admitting that his heart was engaged in such a battle, she only loved him more for his vulnerable honesty.

Men, it turned out, felt deeply. Incredibly so—and that had become a revelation over the years of her marriage. Maybe because she was raised without brothers or because her dad had been a stern man. The never-let-em-see-you-cry type. Helen didn't know for sure. But realizing that her young husband *felt* to the depth of his soul had pried open the deepest places of her own heart for him. Because of that, she came to see that so much of Kevin's struggles with alcohol had been rooted in emotion he didn't know how to deal with. Knowing such had also acted as a catalyst to a level of intimacy with her husband that Helen hadn't known was possible.

Such a beautiful gift, Lord. Thank You for it.

Tyler wrapped his arm around her from the opposite side of where Jacob was. "Dad would tell us to pray."

A stray tear dripped from Helen's eye. "Yes. He would do that. And I suspect you have been."

Jacob and Tyler exchanged a look and nodded. Then Jacob swallowed. "I could never take Dad's place, but—" His deep voice cracked.

Helen rubbed his back. "You have taken your own place. All of you have—and are such fine men. You do know that Dad and I are incredibly proud of you, don't you?"

Tears swam in both boy's eyes.

Jacob sniffed and swallowed again and then bowed his head. "God . . ." His words broke. He drew a new breath and tried again. "My dad, God . . ." The full-grown man who had behaved like a stone for several years while he and Kate were estranged from the family trembled as he held on to Helen.

At her other side, Tyler shifted to lay a comforting grip on Jacob's shoulder. "Yeah, God," Tyler prayed. "You know what's happening with Dad. We're not ready to let him go."

Helen squeezed her closed eyes, and more tears dripped onto her cheeks. Pressing into more than thirty years of faith, she spoke into the aching silence that had settled. "The truth is, Father, we will never be ready to let him go." She gulped back the surge of emotion that threatened to overwhelm her and then pressed on. "Oh, God, give us strength where we are weak, healing where there is brokenness, and grace where our trust falters. Help us to say with Jesus, *Your will be done.* And in this and through it all, no matter what happens next, give us each new faith to know that in good times or in bad, You are always faithful. You are always good."

Both men pressed in closer, and she squeezed them harder.

"Mrs. Murphy?" called a cautious voice from the edge of the waiting room.

Helen stepped back from the small cove her boys had created, swiping tears from her cheeks before she turned to the young man waiting for her response. "I am Helen Murphy."

With walnut-brown hair and nearly golden eyes, somewhere in his mid to late twenties, the medical professional in scrubs reminded her of Brayden. How often had her youngest son been in this young man's shoes—going to talk to the family? Possibly to deliver bad news?

Such a hard, hard thing to do.

Lord, help him as You do us . . .

Helen lifted her chin. "Are you the doctor?"

"I am, ma'am. Dr. Katz." He motioned to a nearby sitting arrangement. "Would you like to sit while we talk for a few moments?"

That couldn't mean anything good, could it? Helen nodded, and her boys flanked her as they all sat. Dr. Katz folded his hands as he leaned his elbows against his knees. "First, your husband is stable for the moment."

A great gust of relief blew from Helen's lungs. She'd been so afraid . . . so certain that the worst had happened. That Kevin was gone. A sob quaked through her frame before she could catch it back. Sniffing, she nodded. "That is good news."

"It is. A great relief, to be honest, because it wasn't looking good for a time." Dr. Katz sat back, his look of concern uneased. "However, we're not clear of danger yet. I'm recommending a transfer to a larger hospital so that a cardiac specialist can see him."

"What do you mean by not clear of danger?" Tyler asked.

"We've given Kevin a clot-busting medication to restore blood flow to the blocked arteries in his heart. As I said, he is stable now, so that seems to have worked. But in a hospital this size, we don't have the ability to determine the extent of damage Kevin's heart has suffered, and he needs to see a cardiologist for definitive care." Dr. Katz pulled in a long breath. "The thing is, I suspect he may need more involved procedures—surgery—to address this heart issue."

"Surgery . . . as in bypass?" Helen asked.

Jacob covered her hand and squeezed.

"Perhaps. But I'm an ER doctor, Mrs. Murphy, not a cardiologist. I've sent our tests on, but in these situations, we always feel it's best to transfer a patient like your husband."

Jacob nodded. "How will you transfer him?"

"We prefer to fly such a case out, especially considering the distance. Nearly three hours is too far for an ambulance transfer."

Helen took it in for a moment. Such good news—Kevin was stable! Moments before, that was everything. But now, hearing he might need surgery—and so close to such trauma—fear sprouted all over again, sending tendrils to clasp her heart and squeeze.

"May I see him first?"

Dr. Katz stood. "Yes, though he's quite sedated. I can't promise he'll know you're there right now."

"Can she ride with him on the transfer?"

This time the doctor shook his head. "I'm afraid that's outside of protocol. With medical staff en route, there is simply not enough room."

Helen stood, and her boys followed, Jacob still gripping her hand. "I can drive. Will they be expecting me once I get there?"

"Yes, I'll see to that." The doctor motioned toward the door that blocked the patient ER rooms. "But I can only have one of you back to see him for the moment."

Tyler rubbed her back and Jacob kissed her knuckles.

"Tell him we're here and we're praying," Ty said.

Helen nodded and followed the young doctor toward the restricted area. When he swiped his badge, the door unlocked and opened, and Dr. Katz allowed her to pass first. "Mrs. Murphy, I am so sorry you have to go through this."

Stopping inside the door, Helen turned and reached for the man's arm. "Thank you for what you do."

"It's my job."

She shook her head. "I have a son about your age. He's a resident in Nashville—at Saint Jude. What you do is more than a job, and if you're anything like Brayden, I know what it does to your heart, to your emotions."

He blinked, as if she'd brushed a nerve, and then nodded. "I'm glad your husband is still with us." Then he turned, leading her to Kevin's room. A curtain hung in the space, portioning off his bed from what could be enough space for two more patient beds. Dr. Katz stopped and drew back the curtain. "A nurse is in with him now, and she'll be in and out. We'll finalize the arrangements for the transfer and let you know a time frame as soon as we can."

Helen nodded, and he moved away. With a quick prayer for strength and stability, she passed through the curtain.

"Kevin," she breathed.

He looked so pale and still. So unlike the strong man who had woken up at five every morning, worked with tools all day long, and came home smelling like sawdust and sweat every evening. Stepping to his side that did not have tubes dripping meds into his arm, Helen slipped her hand into his. His fingers were chilly and unresponsive, but as she studied him, she saw the slight rise and fall of his chest.

"You're still with us," she said, more to herself than anything. Biting her bottom lip, she fought back a sob. "I'd prefer you keep it that way for a while longer, if you please."

Those chilled fingers pressed hers. Not Kevin's normal strong clasp, but enough.

Say you'll stay with me. His plea from so many years ago whispered through her heart.

She'd promised him until death. Standing there at his side, his weak hand holding hers, Helen was so deeply grateful that for now, she had not reached the end of her vow.

It seemed this had happened before, at least in a similar way.

Kevin's hold felt clumsy, his fingers numb and swollen, but he was sure there was a palm in his. He firmed a grip around the smaller hand in his to confirm. The sensation of a touch—her thumb—soothing over the inside of his wrist registered.

"Helen," he mumbled.

His hand lifted as if it was dead weight and then her soft lips pressed against his palm. "I'm here." Her voice was soft and salted with emotion, yet there was strength in her words. "I'm right here with you, love."

Yes. It had happened this way before. Even in the fog of whatever he'd been given during his medical crisis, Kevin remembered the similarities of that time so many years ago. Then as now, he'd woken up to her touch. And then as now, he'd been washed in the relief of her presence. Her faithfulness.

It could have gone so very differently.

Kevin remembered that part with heart-piercing acuity. Thirty-some years ago that terrible moment, for all that was right and fair, *should* have gone differently. Beginning with the fact that he did, in fact, wake up. And not in hell.

And ending with the grace that Helen had held his hand, had stayed with him. God knew, she could have made a different choice. No one would have blamed her—him least of all. He had failed her utterly. What woman deserved a drunk for a husband? What woman would show up to the hospital, tired from mothering two toddlers, carrying her third child, and having come off a late-evening shift at a diner to sit with her damaged husband—and that, broken by his own stupidity?

Against all reason, Helen had.

Kevin swallowed the lump of emotion growing in his throat. He blinked through the haze of lights and blurred reality, searching for the face of his beloved. She didn't come into perfect focus, but he knew the loveliness of her face enough. "Thank you," he rasped.

She moved, fingering the locks of his short hair that had likely matted to his forehead, and then bent to brush his mouth with hers. "No thanks required." She kissed his temple. "Where else would I be?"

He'd not deserved the love of this woman. It amazed him all over again, because though he'd been that fool who had miraculously survived rolling his truck into the banks of Sugar Creek while driving drunk, the fact that she'd stayed with him through those dark years remained stunning.

For all his life, he would not forget that. He'd determined to *always* remember. And so, as Helen kissed his knuckles one more time before the medical people insisted she leave his side, Kevin determined to remember it again.

They moved him to a different bed and belted him in place, all the while using words like *transfer* and *flight* and *cardiologist*. But it all mostly faded to the far reaches of his mind. Once again, history took center stage, and Kevin allowed the overwhelming power of it to reach in deep.

He'd not understood right away. The incessant beeping and constant motion of someone always at his side did not make sense. He had little willpower to understand though, as the overpowering concern was the pain. It sizzled and throbbed through his head and neck. A duller but no less concerning ache pulsed in his leg.

Not a normal hangover, to be sure. Why was the agony in his brain so sharp? And what had he done to his leg?

Twenty-four-year-old Kevin Murphy could not think straight enough to formulate an answer. Not immediately.

But then.

Then the facts whaled upon him with such a vindictive intensity that he'd wished them gone forever in the same instant. Though he'd been wicked drunk, what had happened marched through his pain-seized memory frame by frame, as if he were watching it from an outside point of view.

Keys in his hand, the weak warning sounded in his mind. *Don't go. Not like this.*

He'd told that voice, whatever it was intruding on his inebriated purpose, to shut up. He'd go find his wife. Tell her the way things were—namely that he was coming home and that was the end of it.

You're not fit.

Not fit? To drive? Pshh. He was fine.

For her?

A burning nausea churned in his gut. It made him angry and also made him want to curl up like a little boy and cry.

Kevin did neither. Instead he marched out of his dad's lonely shack of a cabin, slamming the wafer-thin door shut in his wake, and made his way to his truck. The second time he stumbled, that voice touched his mind again. *Don't do this.*

He ignored it.

A full moon lit the narrow highway as he turned onto it. This way was familiar. He'd been traveling it since he'd been driving illegally at the age of fourteen—something he'd started doing by necessity. How else was he going to get to school?

Kevin could drive this road asleep. Or thoroughly sloshed. "I'm fine." He spat the claim into the dark cab, a strangely delayed response to that voice that rankled him.

Nothing responded back. Which was deeply satisfying.

Kevin sagged back against the seat, hooking his forearm over the steering wheel.

Helen would take him back. She had to. He needed her to. Otherwise, what did he have in life? An empty cabin full of crappy memories, both of which he'd like to dump kerosene over and light a match.

The emptiness of that answer threatened to swallow him. Instead, Kevin focused on what he did have with Helen.

As mad as he was with her right then—her kicking him out of his own home and everything—the fact was he *loved* her. Fiercely. Because she'd loved him. Of all the guys she could have been with, and as beautiful and smart and kind as she was, Helen had plenty of choices—she'd chosen to be with him. To promise a lifetime with him.

Being with her made him feel, at least for snippets of time, whole. As he'd never felt that way in his entire life, Kevin desperately clung to those fragments, hoping they'd extend into something lasting. Something better than long spaces of dark abyss. Maybe even eventually they would completely overtake the other feeling. The one of broken emptiness and rejection.

No one else could ever do that for him.

Helen had to take him back. There was just no other way he could survive this life.

Say you'll stay with me...

Emptiness engulfed his heart as his years-old plea echoed. Kevin squeezed his eyes shut as a volatile concoction of desperation, humiliation, insufficiency, and frustration rushed into fill that bleak vacancy.

He'd thought marrying Helen would fix it all.

It hadn't.

Was he going to feel like this forever?

Hopelessness whispered an insidious *yes, forever* just as he opened his eyes.

Up ahead was the S curve in the road. It followed the bend of the river, which ran some fifteen feet below the highway, a rocky embankment separating the two. Kevin knew it was there.

But he didn't turn the wheel.

Oh God! Through the scorching pain knifing through his brain, Kevin's heart cried in horror and agony to a being he didn't even believe in.

He'd done it on purpose.

He'd not turned on purpose.

CHAPTER FOUR

(in which Helen is wrong)

T he drive down the mountain was filled with silence. Helen kept it
     that way. No radio. No one else in the car—she'd insisted her boys
stay back in Sugar Pine. Sent Matt and Ty back home. Called Brayden and
told him not to fly in just yet.

This was between her and God right now.

Fear had a way of holding praise ransom—and by extension, her soul.
Even in the midst of crisis, Helen wanted to be free of it. Otherwise she
would be taken under, held beneath a suffocating layer of panic and hopelessness. Many years ago she'd learned freedom in hope—and it had been
a hard-fought lesson. One she and Kevin had battled for with everything
they had.

And the hope was this: *Christ in me.* And her anchor, *in all her ways,
every moment of every day*, know *Him*.

Life was uncertain, but God was unchanging. He was always good and
always able. Tomorrow could bring joy or sorrow, ease or pain—sometimes
both at once. But God's love never failed. And she and Kevin were held safe
in that abiding love, hidden in Christ with God.

God had brought them through such a rocky beginning. He'd delivered
her from hopelessness and Kevin out of the claws of addiction. By His love
and grace, He'd blessed them with seven boys. Seven! Through every crisis
that had come up after that—and there had been more than a few—God
had provided.

Even so, as she faced Kevin's possible heart surgery, Helen's heart trembled.

With both hands, she gripped the cool steering wheel as she blinked against the streams of tears. Here, in the shelter of her vehicle, when it was just her and her Savior, she could let the rivers flow.

It'd be forty years that Christmas Eve. Forty years as Kevin's wife—and most of them good.

As she rejoiced in that unlikely fact, Helen considered how different this moment of crisis was from the one so long ago. How, though her heart ached and she did ask God for more time—for Him to let Kevin live through this—she didn't do so with such despair as she had back then.

Or with a disturbingly divided heart.

Thirty-some years ago that had not been the case. When she'd picked up the phone at the diner near the end of her shift, certain it was her babysitter calling, but had instead heard Dave's voice on the other line, she had been plunged into such a myriad of confusing emotions that she couldn't even put them to words.

She hadn't wanted Kevin to die.

But how could he be so stupid—driving drunk? She didn't want their marriage to fail—but she couldn't see them lasting either. Not the way they were going. She didn't want her boys to not have their father. But she wasn't going to raise them with a drunk dad around.

There was no way out. No way forward. There was only devastating failure. *Or...*

Shame had pierced her heart as she'd driven toward the hospital that night so long ago. Because she wondered if this *was* the out she had timidly asked Dave's God for.

What a horrible thing to think.

See, she'd thought to Mrs. Clayton, who had gone to stay with the boys and was not in the car with her while she sped her way to the emergency room. *I'm a terrible person. God doesn't want someone like me.*

And then she attempted to banish her shame by burying any thoughts about Kevin doing anything other than surviving his wreck. She determined to stay right there with him. At his side, loving him no matter what.

But please, she'd petitioned that God she wasn't sure would listen to such an ugly heart as hers. *Please change things. Make him stop drinking* . . .

At the time Helen didn't have a name for those thoughts she'd sent to what she'd considered the ether. She certainly wouldn't have called them prayers. Nor did she really have any hope that the cry of her heart would be not only heard but moved upon.

But there were people who prayed for her and for Kevin. Dave and his family had been doing so for several years, and that fateful night, Helen had discovered much later, they were literally on their knees in her trailer house, keeping watch over her sons, interceding for Kevin and Helen with all their hearts.

There are moments in life that are pivotal.

Helen hadn't realized that night, while she'd held her unconscious husband's hand and wept about a future that looked bleak, that night was their shifting point. Something momentous had begun.

But all these years later, she saw it. Plain as anything. Like Jesus with the men who brought their lame friend to him, God had heard the pleas of her faith-filled friends and had moved.

Kevin survived his drunken car wreck. With a broken leg and a split skull, he was sent home to recover—a process that involved him *not* drinking for the first time since he was thirteen years old. His boss at the mill offered for him to work in the office while he couldn't work out on the floor—an undeserved kindness that met more of the Murphys' needs than anyone realized.

There, Kevin had learned how to run a business.

On the condition that he join AA, he'd also been invited into the owner's carpentry shop, because he could still swing a hammer. He could still learn how to read a blueprint. How to take a stick of wood and create something new and useful from it. There Kevin discovered a passion for building. Little did he know, but that would be the conception of a new career.

During that time, Helen continued to work a few evenings and Saturday mornings at the diner, because hospital bills were expensive, and they had more coming. Kevin stayed home with their two boys while she did so. He became truly *Daddy* to his boys.

Helen pulled into the hospital parking lot just as a particular poignant memory filled her mind.

She came home from the diner late, as often happened on a Friday night, and found Kevin already in bed—also not uncommon.

She'd taken a quick shower to rinse the smell of grease and coffee from the diner off her body, then put on a nightgown, brushed her teeth, and slipped in between the sheets next to him. As soon as she was settled against the mattress, Kevin had turned onto his side and hauled her in close. Several months had passed since his accident—his cast was gone, head fully healed, and her belly was swollen with their third child, due within weeks. Even so, Helen tucked herself against him as snug as she could and shut her eyes. But as she drifted into sleep, she felt him shudder.

"Kevin?" She tipped her chin up, searching for his face in the dark. "You okay?"

His hold around her tightened. "I took the boys to the cabin this evening."

"Oh?" Helen couldn't imagine why he had done that. He hated it there. Wanted to burn the place down, but as it was in the middle of the forest, that was ill advised. Instead, the shack that had housed his childhood remained abandoned. A haunting monument to all that was wrong in his life.

"The county says I have to do something with it."

"Oh." It was the late eighties, and commuting from a tiny, almost ghost mountain town was nearly a decade away from being trendy. That meant that there wasn't much use for a shack in the hills—no sell value at all.

But doing something with it would involve money. And for Kevin, a steep sum of emotion. The Murphys could afford neither.

"But that's not—" His whisper cut off in raw emotion. "Matt just held my hand and talked about the squirrels and the trees. He smiled and tossed sticks. Like . . . like life is good. And when we were leaving, I was buckling Jacob in his seat, and he grabbed my face with both of his chubby little hands. He smiled and said—" This time a full sob shook Kevin's body. "He said, 'I wuv you, 'addy.'"

Helen slipped her hand up his chest and curved it around his neck, holding his head against hers.

"They just love me, Helen," he whispered through tears.

"Yes." She kissed his wet cheek. "They do."

"And you—" He cupped her jaw, smoothed his thumb along her cheek-bone. "You're still here. With me."

Helen nodded.

"You didn't have to stay with me. I don't know why you did."

She swallowed against a lump in her throat.

"But you're here." He exhaled a quivering breath. "I'm still alive, and my sons love me even though I haven't been a good dad, and you're still here with me even though you had every reason to leave." Kevin tucked her back in close against his chest, holding her as if she was a gift to be cherished. "God must be real. And He must be good, because those are miracles."

In the darkness, held against him, her own tears flowed.

"Helen?" Kevin whispered tentatively.

"Yes, love."

"I want to try life Dave's way."

She wasn't sure what that meant exactly and didn't know what to say. It couldn't be a bad thing though. Dave was a good man. And he'd been such a faithful friend to them both.

After a space of silence, Kevin whispered, "I want to go to church on Sunday."

Helen leaned back against his arms, once again searching for his face in the dark. She couldn't think of a time when he'd shocked her more.

His hand cupped her face again, thumb tracing her brow. "Will you come with me?"

"Yes." Her response was more wonder than excitement.

Truth be told, church made her feel wildly uncomfortable. Not because it was unfamiliar—quite the contrary. She'd grown up in church. The kind where only long skirts and brown shoes were acceptable attire. It had been a place where no smiling was allowed, and people scurried away as quickly as they could once the service was over. She remembered it as a cold, unwelcoming place that was attended by dutiful souls as a sign of their virtue.

Helen hadn't gone since she'd married Kevin. Because it was uncomfortable.

"I don't know how to be," Kevin said. "Will you help me?"

"Kevin . . ."

"Please, Helen. I need you in this."

"I'm not saying no." With a palm to his chest, she pressed back a little more. "But I don't know how to be, either. Church never made much sense to me."

She wasn't a good enough person to be sitting in a pew before the judgment of God, and clearly by her lingering discomfort, God wasn't keen on her return.

Kevin sighed.

"It doesn't mean we shouldn't try it," she said into his disappointment.

He held still for several more beats, and Helen could feel his hope plummeting. "Kevin, we'll go. Maybe it'll be different than I remember."

His arms came around her and drew her in again. "There's got to be something in it. Dave is . . ." He didn't finish.

"Dave is a good man." Helen finished for him. "His parents are good people."

Kevin nodded against her.

Helen swallowed. "Okay," she whispered. And didn't speak the rest of her thoughts. They went something like, *The Claytons are good people—that's why church works for them.*

Strange how as she parked under a streetlamp not far from the ER entrance at the city hospital, that thirty-five-year-old thought was such a clear memory to Helen. It made her chuckle—a sad sort of laugh at her sad little view.

Thank God she'd discovered that she'd been so very wrong. Not about the Claytons being good people—they were. But about church, and by extension her entire view of God.

Praise God she'd been so very wrong. And even more so, that He was determined to prove it.

CHAPTER FIVE

(in which by the faith of a few good friends . . .)

K evin felt a portion of his tension unfurl as Helen slipped her hand into his. His mind was still cloudy, body still ached, but his wife was there beside him again.

He'd married her as a young, foolish man. More selfish than anything. Now he loved her as a grateful man, one who knew he hadn't deserved her and who was determined to love this gift God had bestowed upon him.

Unfortunately, lying there in a hospital bed with tubes running into his veins, he felt a little helpless and frustrated that there his wife was again, bearing up strong for him. He'd prefer more than anything not to put her through this. But here they were.

"The damage to your heart is surprisingly minimal." Dr. Agate paused, locked up from his screen, and offered a wisp of a smile. "I'd expected significantly more after I spoke with Dr. Katz. How long did it take to get you from your job site to the hospital?"

Kevin had no idea. "You'd have to ask my son," he mumbled.

"It doesn't matter that much, I guess." The doctor returned to studying whatever was on his portable screen—likely Kevin's medical notes sent down from Sugar Pine Community Hospital. "Like I said, I expected more damage. As a cautionary note, I will say that once I get in there for bypass, I might see something that will change my initial assessment, but from these scans, I really think we're looking at well under twenty percent. Like closer to ten percent."

Helen squeezed Kevin's hand. "What does that mean?"

"A damaged heart doesn't recover well. If you lose twenty percent, that damaged portion is pretty much gone."

"Oh." Helen sat back, her expression frightened.

Kevin didn't like this man scaring his wife. "But what is the outlook on ten percent damage?"

The doctor looked up again, glancing first at Helen and then focused on Kevin. "Well, at twenty percent loss, we have some significant lifestyle changes to address. Your heart won't function like it used to, and you'll get tired faster. Out of breath sooner. You'll have to slow down, maybe change your working habits."

"But you think the damage is more like ten percent."

"I do."

"Then?"

"You'll be looking at something closer to your old normal." The man spoke so . . . clinically. As if this was all academic.

Kevin's life was not academic. He had a family. A wife he loved to please. Sons he was determined to keep up with. A business he'd built from the ground up with his own two hands. What did *closer to your old normal* mean? Was he going to be able to swing a hammer on a daily basis? Hike the back trail with his boys when they came home? Toss a ball with his grandkids? Make love to his wife?

He turned his head to look at Helen. She'd recomposed herself—the wild panic in her expression now soft and calm.

Her thumb brushed over his wrist. "We'll take it as it comes, love. For now, let's get through what's next."

Lifting her hand to his lips, he brushed a kiss across her knuckles, then pressed her fingers to his cheeks. Then he looked back at the stiff doctor. "What is next?"

"Bypass surgery." Keeping his sterile, distant tone, Dr. Agate lowered his screen and sat on the rolling chair opposite Helen. "The good news is that we have the ability to perform a minimally invasive bypass in this facility. That will significantly decrease your recovery time, and you're a good candidate for the procedure. However, there are risks. You'll be on a ventilator while in surgery. We'll most likely take a healthy blood vessel from inside your chest wall and use it to redirect the blood flow around your damaged artery."

"That sounds . . . complicated," Helen said.

Finally, a touch of humanness entered the doctor's expression. "I know it sounds scary. But the success rate is very high. And without it, Kevin is at a higher risk for a repeat heart attack in the future, because there is blockage in the artery. The blood vessel will act as an alternative unclogged passage for the blood to move freely around the blocked artery. It really is your best option. And as I said, the ability to do a minimally invasive version of the bypass is truly good news for you."

Kevin processed this news in the moments of quiet that passed in the room. Then, "How soon does this need to happen."

"You're here now. I'd recommend we get you in the OR within the next twenty-four hours."

He blinked, pressing back into the stiff mattress of the hospital bed. Not what he'd expected. He'd hoped to put off such a major operation until after Christmas. After their fortieth anniversary.

Couldn't they do it that way?

"The sooner the better," Helen said.

Kevin shifted his eyes to his wife. "But the kids are all coming . . ."

She stood and kissed his head. "At this point, they'd be coming either way. We'd all feel better if you were fully on the road to recovery rather than waiting for such a big operation."

"But . . ." But he had plans. Big ones, to surprise Helen with. Plans he couldn't see through if he was in the hospital for the next week and then on restrictions for the few following that.

"I believe this is the best course, Mr. Murphy." Dr. Agate stood. "I'll give you a few moments to process."

Kevin waited until the click of the door closing sounded in the room. "Helen, this isn't what I wanted."

She chuckled softly. "I can't imagine anyone ever wanted a heart attack."

"But I'm stable. Dr. Katz said so. We could delay—"

"There's no reason to do that."

Yes, there was. She thought the boys and their families were all coming for Christmas—and she was thrilled about it. But that wasn't the only reason they'd all made plans for this year.

Maybe he could still pull it off. After all, he did have seven grown, capable sons. And six—nearly seven—lovely, capable daughters-in-love. They'd be willing to help, certainly.

Could it still happen? With all of his not-functioning-correctly heart, he wanted it to.

"I don't know what you're thinking right now." Helen sat back and crossed her arms, a knowing look filling her expression. "Or, rather more likely, scheming. But I'm going to demand something, and you can't argue. Get your heart fixed, Kevin. That's what I want for Christmas. It's *all* I want."

Helen was hardly ever demanding. Full of ideas, yes. But not demanding. And even if she was, Kevin had been powerless to deny her much of anything.

Because he loved his darling wife. Whatever she wanted had always become his goal. Making her smile at him was always his favorite achievement.

So then, he'd get his broken heart fixed. For Helen.

ele

"Why would God do that?" Twenty-five-year-old Kevin sat at a table with Dave and Mr. Clayton—a man who had done as much as he could over the past ten years to be a father to Kevin. It was not lost on Kevin how much this moment must have been a hope to both men. Sitting there together, each with a Bible opened in front of them. Kevin listening, trying to understand.

And he was trying.

Step two: I admit there is a Power greater than me, and He is able to restore me to sanity.

Kevin had embraced that, along with the other twelve steps. Especially after he'd encountered the unbelievable moment in realizing he was in the midst of miracles. His life, the love in it, his family, and his friends . . . That he still had all those beautiful gifts despite his recklessness was an absolute miracle.

Getting over that was not an option. Kevin didn't want to get over it. He wanted to live in utter wonder of it. To let it seep in every day and float gratitude into his life. With humble desperation, Kevin wanted his life changed by it.

Irreversibly transformed by this God who Dave and Mr. Clayton loved—the very One Kevin believed was real and active, even if he couldn't fully grasp all the things in the Bible.

Like this. Kevin rubbed his brow as he glanced back at Genesis 2. "Why would God plant temptation in the middle of paradise?"

George Clayton nodded slowly, as if he understood the resistance Kevin felt against this move on God's part. It seemed . . . like a setup. Like that moment Kevin's dad had set a beer in front of him when he'd been thirteen, grinned cynically, and walked away. It'd been a silent taunting dare: _Just try not to be like me, boy. Think you're better? I dare you—just try it._

Angry and confused, Kevin had gotten up and walked away, only to have curiosity overcome him within an hour. And within that same hour, he'd experienced his first buzz. And his dad had laughed.

For whatever twisted reason that had possessed him, Tom Murphy had wanted his son to fail. To that very day, the blistering pain of that fact resided deep within Kevin's heart.

But for all that Kevin could see in his life now, he believed that God was good. He wasn't cruel or selfish—not like Kevin's own father had been. But this tree of knowledge of good and evil?

"I think it's pretty easy to *only* look at that forbidden tree," Mr. Clayton began quietly. "But let's start where God started. He said, *You are* free *to eat of* any *tree in the garden.* There was beautiful abundance in that. Great freedom. Truly they would have lacked no good thing."

Kevin nodded. "I can see that. But why put the *one* there—the forbidden?"

"I think perhaps it was to hold out a choice," Dave replied. "As if God was telling Adam, *Live in my abundance. Choose to love me, to trust me.* And the way Adam could choose that love and trust was to obey God. That's only really possible if there is a choice one way or the other."

"But He must have known that they would make the wrong decision." Kevin squirmed in his chair, not wanting to accuse God of something bad, even if that was exactly what it seemed.

"Since I believe God is all knowing, yes, I'd say you're right." Mr. Clayton leaned forward, eyebrows drawn in. "But He still offered the choice. I think that's what love does. It doesn't demand, but invites. God could have offered no choice, but instead He held out the dangerous invitation to love or to turn away."

Step three: I must make a decision to turn my will and my life over to the care of God.

Kevin still couldn't fully comprehend this great gamble on God's part. It seemed easier to only offer safe abundance, no other options. But then, Kevin was not God.

And maybe, for at least that moment, in this study with these men, that was the point.

"Kevin!" Mrs. Clayton burst into the dining room, her cheeks rosy and eyes bright. "You boys have to wrap this up. Helen just called, and you have to go!"

Heart ramping up to a sprint, Kevin shut the Bible the Claytons had given him a few weeks before and nearly knocked the chair beneath him over as he scrambled up. "The baby?"

Biting her lip, Elizabeth Clayton nodded with a grin. "The baby. I'm going with you, and you'll leave me at your place with the boys."

Ten hours, forty-seven minutes later Connor Michael Murphy made his debut. Seven pounds, four ounces, dark hair like Kevin's, and big curious eyes that took in everything new about him, Connor barely made a peep. He cried for a moment—Kevin was sure the nurse had pinched the baby to force a sound out of his brand-new son. But as soon as the warm washing water touched his wet, matted hair, Connor's soft wails ended, and he simply took in life.

Cleaned and swaddled, the nurse passed the warm bundle of life into Kevin's arms.

There were no words.

Though Connor was his third son, the truth was this was the first birth Kevin was clear minded and more in wonder than utter terror when he first held his newborn. Connor gazed up at him, complete trust in those beautiful eyes, and a wave of awe washed over Kevin.

Had love ever seemed this big?

Kevin squeezed his eyes shut and let himself drown in it.

Step seven: humbly ask God to remove all my shortcomings.

Nothing had ever seemed so important in his life. Arms wrapped secure around this miracle of his son, Kevin bowed his head until he could smell the fresh newness of life. *God, take all my failures. For the sake of this child. And my other boys. For Helen. Make me a new man—a better one.*

In the thirty-six years since Connor had been born, Kevin had not forgotten that prayer. As he prepared his heart, in the space of solitary quiet given him before his bypass surgery, he pondered that moment afresh.

Only a couple of weeks before Connor's birth, Dave had led Kevin to Christ by showing him that repentance and faith was all Jesus had asked for. It had seemed so ridiculously simple—to believe on the Lord Jesus Christ and be saved. But in that simplicity, Kevin had discovered a power outside of himself. The acknowledgment, as the second step to recovery stated, that there was a Power beyond himself—which required the first step, that Kevin admitted he was, in fact, powerless over alcohol and his life had become unmanageable.

It had *always* been unmanageable—which had been why Kevin had always felt desperation clawing against his soul. That had been the reason he had not turned the wheel that awful night. He chose to wreck because he was so entirely out of control.

It'd been a hard admission. But one that had led him to that moment, holding his brand-new baby boy and asking God to make him new.

Perhaps that was a reason Kevin had struggled so much over the past two years as he'd watched Connor—that baby boy grown up—lose Sadie and dive into the agony of such grief. Kevin's life had been changed dramatically when Connor had been born, and from that moment on he'd worked daily to be different. Prayed daily for grace to be his way out of unmanageable chaos and into a life worth living. Kevin's daily aim had been to live a godly life before his sons so they wouldn't have to experience the web of madness that Kevin had nearly died within.

He had asked so many times over the years for God's protection over his sons. Sadie's death had seemed like an unreasonable *no*. It had spiraled Kevin back to that confusing place he'd been in during the Genesis Bible study, when he'd asked, *Why would God do that?*

Some days Kevin felt like the answer Dave had given him was good enough. God offered the choice to love. To obey. To live in His abundance rather than looking with envy at what had been kept away.

Other times, though, the *why* seemed unfathomable. And it made all the other whys seems just as empty and dark.

Why Sadie? Why Connor? Why Reid?

And they'd harken back the other unanswered whys: Why Jackson's cleft palate? Why Jacob's hardness? Why Tyler's fall? Why Brayden's rebellion?

And those were just a few, about his children. There had been others over the years as well. Big, hard moments for which, honestly, there were still no satisfying answers.

Like, why Dave?

As that question resurfaced, pain squeezed Kevin's chest. A reoccurring ache that had ebbed and flowed over the years whenever his mind drifted toward his best friend.

There simply wasn't an answer. But there was a soft presence and the words of Psalm 116 whispered in Mrs. Clayton's tear-laden voice several weeks after her only child had been buried.

Return to your rest, oh my soul, for the Lord has dealt bountifully with you. A broken praise if ever there was one.

And so moments before he was to have his heart stopped so that it could be repaired, Kevin echoed the words of his faithful friend's mother.

"Return to your rest, oh my soul, for the Lord has dealt bountifully with you."

CHAPTER SIX

(in which love extends through years and absence)

"Oh my goodness." Helen stood from her seat in the waiting room. "How did you know to come?"

Aided by a cane, Elizabeth Clayton made her way across the sterile space, her posture as erect as ever, her mouth set determinedly, kindness in her eyes. "Jacob called me. Of course, I came."

The moment those thin arms gathered her close, Helen rested her head against Elizabeth's shoulder. "Oh, Beth," she whispered, "why do we keep meeting in a waiting room?"

"Sweet girl." Elizabeth leaned back and cupped Helen's cheek. "Life is but a waiting room, isn't it?"

Helen blinked against tears. "I'm not ready . . ."

"No. But Kevin is much more ready now than he was so many years ago. That is a comfort."

Pursing her quivering lips, Helen nodded.

"And anyway, the prospect of 'goodbye for now' is much less than it was yesterday, right?"

"It is." Perhaps one less familiar with Elizabeth Clayton would think her words were cold or insensitive. They were not, however, and Helen knew it.

This woman who had acted as a mother to both Kevin and her at a time when Kevin had no parents and hers had turned away, had borne her own griefs. Elizabeth Clayton did not offer rosy encouragement out of ignorance but held out true hope from a heart that had gone through the waters of heartache and found that, as Isaiah 43 had promised, the Lord had been with her.

As He would be with Helen come what may.

Helen looped an arm through the crook of Elizabeth's elbow, and side by side the pair stepped back to the chairs. As they sat down, a gentle quiet settled with them—Elizabeth had never been one for too many words—and Helen allowed her memory to travel back.

The phone call came from George. "Helen, I know it's late and the kids are in bed. But we need your prayers."

Over the past ten years, Kevin and Helen had met often with the Claytons. The couple, and Dave, had taken them into their hearts as family. Asking for prayer was not unusual. But a phone call at nearly ten at night asking for such was.

"Should I get Kevin?"

"You can pass it along. I need to go. Dave—" George's voice broke, and Helen's heart dropped into her stomach. "Dave has been in an accident."

Knocked breathless, Helen dropped onto a chair at the kitchen table. "Oh no."

"He's being life-flighted out to a bigger hospital." Again, George paused to draw in a shuddering breath. "It doesn't look good, Helen."

"I'll pray. I'll tell Kevin, and we'll both pray." That ended the call. Helen told Kevin, as well as called her mom, who had come around to trusting Kevin as a sober man by then. As soon as Mom arrived to stay with the boys—six of them at that time—she and Kevin left. It took three hours to get to the hospital.

Dave was already gone by the time they met George and Elizabeth in the waiting room.

"What happened?" Helen whispered.

Through tear-laden eyes, Elizabeth looked at Kevin cautiously. As if she didn't want to say it for fear that Kevin's heart might shatter. *Leave it to the woman to worry about Kevin's heart when hers was broken.*

George stared at his feet and shook his head. "Head-on collision. Hit by a . . . a drunk driver."

The impact of the horrible irony was immediate, and Kevin nearly collapsed with the weight of it. Nearly, but for George, whose ready arms caught him and held him fast, and the pair sobbed.

It was an awful day. One of the worst Kevin and Helen had ever known. Certainly *the* worst for George and Elizabeth Clayton.

Helen waited in that very hospital now. And no, Elizabeth's wise, hopeful words weren't the stilted pie-in-the-sky sort. She was truly one who could say, with Horatio Spafford in the midst of heartbreak, *It is well, it is well, with my soul.*

And having her there as Helen waited for news of Kevin's surgery, aged hand holding hers, lent great strength. Enough for Helen to murmur those gut-twisting words of that powerful old hymn. "Whatever my lot, thou hast taught me to say . . ."

The hand that held hers squeezed, and Elizabeth added her gentle voice to Helen's weak one. "It is well, it is well, with my soul."

She wished George was there with them. With his rich baritone, he would give harmony to the words. Though she couldn't explain why, music always added a richness to words already steeped with meaning. Music had a power all its own—a way to move the soul.

But George wasn't with them and wouldn't be coming. He had gone to his Savior the year Brandon had graduated high school. Had it been ten years? Goodness, time went by. After George died, Elizabeth had moved toward the coast to be closer to her younger brother and his family. Dave had never married or had children, so it made sense for Elizabeth to move closer to her only remaining family, but Helen had always ached at losing the closeness of such a dear friend.

Clearly, however, love extended beyond time and absence.

For a long stretch of time, the two women sat in silence. There was such easy comfort with Elizabeth, and Helen was so grateful for it.

"I was thinking on the drive over about Jackson," Elizabeth said after some ten minutes or so.

Helen looked at her friend, finding that age had produced several more wrinkles on the woman's face, but it had not robbed her of the joyful beauty that had always marked Elizabeth. "Jackson?"

"Yes. I was remembering when he was born. There was so much emotion in that time, wasn't there?"

Even some thirty-four years later, Helen's heart squeezed with a surge of that leftover emotion. It'd been such a potent concoction of fear and anger all mixed in with the joy at the birth of another child.

Helen hadn't known anything about cleft palate before Jackson's birth, other than it happened rarely. To other people's babies. Her first response had been to wonder what she'd done wrong. Poor diet while she was pregnant? Had she taken something bad that had damaged her infant? Following that crushing sense of guilt, she'd panicked over what Jackson's life would look like.

Surgeries—likely multiple times throughout his childhood. Ear and sinus challenges. Speech problems. Self-esteem issues. All of them made the doctor's list of things to be aware of going forward. This, followed by what seemed like an obligatory "Don't worry, though, Mrs. Murphy. Most children with this defect go on to live a perfectly healthy, normal life."

Don't worry? Her son had been born with his lip and palate incomplete. How was she going to feed him? How could she possibly sleep for the next several months before his first surgery to close the gap? And what if he did have hearing loss? She didn't know how to navigate any of that. And this doctor, after giving her a list of what seemed grave warnings, was now saying *don't worry*? As if that was possible.

"I was such a mess," Helen said.

"You had good reason to be." Elizabeth patted her hand.

With a quiet chuckle, Helen hung her head. "I was so afraid that he'd be such a lonely boy. Rejected and made fun of by others. Sad, quiet, and awkward. I kept thinking, *Kids can be so mean*, and I became such a mama bear."

"Mothers are supposed to protect their babies."

"Oh, I was over the top." Helen rubbed her neck as it heated. "Do you know, the thing Kevin and I fought about most as we were raising the boys was Jackson. He kept telling me the boy was fine. I was certain he was being cavalier. We did some serious rounds about it several times over." She shook her head. "In the end Kevin had been right all along. Jackson was absolutely fine. For whatever difficulties he had as a little kid because of his mouth, his massive personality overcame them all. And to think, all that time I thought he'd be a wallflower." Helen snorted a laugh. "Now he makes a living as a stand-up comedian."

Elizabeth winked. "God has a sense of humor."

A touch of comfort warmed Helen's heart. "He does. And God gave Jackson everything he needed in life."

That slim hand patted Helen's. "He does that."

Helen shifted to face Elizabeth more squarely. "How did you get through it, Beth?"

By the shadow of sadness that passed through the older woman's eyes, Helen knew Elizabeth understood her question, and the loss still hurt. Helen couldn't imagine losing a son, and she certainly didn't think a parent ever got over it.

"Day by day." Elizabeth sighed softly and gazed out the window across the room. "At first I wanted the darkness to just swallow me whole. I couldn't fathom going forward in life. And I was mad, secretly." She tapped her chest. "In here. Mad that God would take the only son He'd given me. That He would leave George and me without a family, without a legacy." In her pause, Elizabeth looked at her hands, now folded in her lap. After several heartbeats, she drew in a new breath and looked back at Helen. "But after a time, He made something clear to me." She blinked, and a sheen glazed her eyes.

"What was it?" Helen whispered.

"You." She reached for Helen's hand. "He gave us you and Kevin and the boys. And He had done it through Dave, so in a way you were sort of my son's testimony to me. His testimony of God's goodness, even when it certainly did not feel good."

Helen leaned forward and wrapped her arms around her dear friend. "We always thought you were God's gift to us, not the other way around."

Elizabeth kissed Helen's cheek and leaned back. "You were the reason we stayed in Sugar Pine after Dave died. We loved being a part of your lives. A part of your family. If you want to know the truth, I didn't want to go live with my brother's family after George died."

"We would have had you, Beth!"

"I know it." She patted Helen's hand. "But Caleb was so insistent. And there was purpose in my going there too. His children are also a delight to me, and I get to hold my great-nieces and watch them grow, just as I did your boys." Sitting back, a small smile played at her lips. "Though it may seem small and quiet, I have lived a rich life."

"I think that has a lot to do with you deciding to see it that way."

Elizabeth caught Helen's gaze and held it for a moment. It seemed like a silent passing on of wisdom, a wordless commission for Helen to choose for herself how she would see life. After a breath, Elizabeth rubbed Helen's shoulder and turned forward to gaze out the window again.

"Return to your rest, oh my soul." The woman spoke so softly Helen could barely make out the verse. "For the Lord has been good to you."

He'd expected the first face he would encounter when he blinked awake again to be Helen's. It was not, but this one was nearly as comforting.

"Beth . . ." he rasped.

Though her lips wobbled, the old woman smiled a closed-lip sort of grin. "My dear boy."

"I thought you might come."

"Of course I did." She slipped her hand into his.

Summoning enough strength to do so, Kevin raised that thin hand and pressed it against his cheek. For a long moment, he simply savored the warmth of her skin against his. This motherly touch had been denied him all his childhood but was freely given now, as if a gift of redemption.

"I never told you." He lifted his eyes to meet hers and found the warm kindness of devotion looking back at him. "But you became the mother to me that I never had. I love you for it."

Her throat spasmed as she visibly swallowed. She took several moments before she could speak, and when she did, emotion trembled in her voice. "And you became a son of my heart, Kevin. Mine and George's. And we both have loved you and Helen as if you were our very own."

She sniffed and straightened her posture. "Now then."

A slight grin lifted Kevin's mouth. "Now then. You're still coming, right?"

The gleam of a conspirator entered her eyes. "It's still on?"

"Of course it is."

"I wouldn't miss it." She squeezed his hand and then slipped it from his. "Have you spoken to the boys?"

"They know."

"They must do more now than know." With a firm nod, Elizabeth took charge. "I will call Matthew as soon as I leave this hospital."

"I can talk to him. We'll iron it all out."

"You will not." Her lifted brow said firmly *do not argue with me*. It was a look that apparently all women held in their armory, as he'd witnessed it on his wife's face more times than he could number. "You have seven capable boys. And you have me." With one more firm nod, she leaned over the side of the bed and planted a kiss on his cheek. "You rest. Get well. Nothing more. That's an order."

A chuckle moved through Kevin's chest, which was uncomfortable but somehow still lifted his spirit.

Elizabeth stood, her rise slow but certain as she pressed against her cane. "And now that we have straightened that out, I believe your wife is waiting." Having shuffled a few feet away, the woman stopped and glanced over her shoulder at him. "I'm not sure why she sent me to see you first."

Kevin smiled, because he could guess—Helen knew the gaping hole not having a mother had left in his heart. God had mended that through Elizabeth Clayton. What better time to remind him of God's gracious provisions than when he came through the mending of his physical heart?

"Thank you, Beth," he said.

A lopsided smile lifted her mouth, and then she made her way out of the room.

CHAPTER SEVEN

(in which the future must change)

Kevin sat at the kitchen table, slumped in the chair, laptop open in front of him, a pad of graphing paper and a pencil to the right of it. A cup of weak cinnamon and bay-leaf tea sat at his right hand—the kind Helen made for household members who were unwell. He had never been a fan of it and rarely had need to sip the stuff.

He'd been drinking it way too much the past week. It had gotten old real fast.

A growl of impatience nearly rumbled from his throat. Would have if he'd not gulped it back with a mouthful of that steaming bland tea.

He should not be sitting there. This time of day he should be in the shop, should be hammering something or cutting something or doing something useful with his hands. Not sitting there like a useless man taking up space while his wife worked away at *her* thriving business and his son made sure *Kevin's* business stayed afloat. Instead, he was reconciling work orders that had apparently already been seen to. He scribbled away on a notepad, doodling a project he wouldn't be able to see through to the end.

That wasn't doing the work, and it frustrated Kevin to be sidelined. How was he going to survive the six weeks rest prescribed?

Helen had said Tyler was taking care of the business. Truthfully, Kevin had no doubt that Tyler could handle it, that he *was* handling it. Ty was more than capable, and in the near future—nearer than Kevin had wanted, it seemed—he'd take it over entirely.

The thing was, Kevin wasn't ready to let it go.

The click of the latch at the front door sounded only moments before someone entered the house.

"Hey, Dad." Tyler shut the entry behind him, then strode toward the dining room table. Wearing the dark-gray puffer coat that had duct tape to cover the rips and tears the fabric had suffered over the years of construction work, and walking with a barely perceptible limp, Tyler approached Kevin with a paper hot cup in each hand. "What are you doing here?"

Heat crept up Kevin's neck, as if he'd been caught doing something wrong. Maybe because he felt caught. Caught in a moment of wallowing in self-pity. Caught feeling lost about what life was supposed to look like next.

Clearing his throat, he straightened and looked up at his son with a half a grin, hoping that would convince Ty all was well. No pity party happening there. "Just reconciling some orders. How are things at the shop?"

Tyler set down a paper cup full of something hot and hopefully tastier than the weak tea Kevin been nursing the past hour.

"What did you bring me here?" Kevin asked.

Tyler pulled out the chair across from Kevin and lowered himself onto it as if he might be a bit sore. He dropped a conspirator's wink. "Coffee It's decaf though, so don't get too excited."

Kevin nodded and reached for that small forbidden gift. "I'll take what I can get." After a long drag of the Storm Café's rich brew, he sighed with satisfaction. "Your mother has banned me from all of it."

"I've heard." Tyler grinned and then shrugged. "She loves you and seems to want you to hang around awhile longer. I can't imagine Becca would do much of anything different if it were me." He held up his own coffee, a silent, secret pact of loyalty in the gesture, and Kevin clunked his against it.

"Let's go back to what it is you're doing here." Tyler tapped the pad of paper sitting in front of Kevin. "This doesn't look like order reconciliation—and by the way, that's already been done. Lauren and Jade took a pass at it while you were still in recovery. Both of them being very good at business and all things spreadsheet, I would trust that they did a good job."

Suddenly this visit felt less like a reprieve from the doldrums of recovery and more like the build-up to a mild rebuke. Or something equally unpleasant. Kevin cleared the growing lump from his throat. "I noticed it all looked good."

Once again Tyler tapped that pad of paper. "Now, back to this. What is it?"

Oh, yes. The thing that made Kevin wrestle with frustration and then feel caught when Tyler had entered unexpectedly. Kevin picked up the pencil and traced over the lines he'd sketched, darkening the ones he wanted to keep. "It's a drawing."

"For what?" By his tone, Tyler already had an idea of the answer—and likely he was right.

Kevin squared his gaze directly on his son, taking back his fatherly poise. "For that Henton project. We need a solid sketch and a reasonable materials list before we can put in the bid they asked for."

"Dad." In the space before Tyler plunged forward, the expression in his eyes shifted. When he continued, his voice softened. "Dad, I already turned that job down."

"What?" He shouldn't be surprised or upset. But he was both. "We haven't discussed it."

"It wasn't even a real decision, Dad. We could *not* take that job."

"Hentons would give us a few weeks' grace. It's a big job, Ty. Good money."

"Yeah. It is a big job. One that's remote and a two-hour drive from here."

"We've done that before. Many times over."

Tyler sighed as he wrapped both large hands around his half-full cup. He stared at the space between his arms and slowly nodded. "We have done so before." He peeked at Kevin, hesitancy marking every feature of his expression. "We can't keep doing this though."

"What?" Dread sank into Kevin's gut. This was not simply a mild rebuke, a *Hey, Dad, you really do need to take it easy for a few weeks.* No, this was so much bigger than that.

"*I* can't keep doing this."

Kevin opened his mouth to argue that he'd recover and they'd go on as normal, but then Tyler's statement sank in. *He* couldn't keep doing this? "I . . . I don't understand. Is . . . is it your leg? Does it bother you?"

"That's not it. My leg is as fine as it was last year. And the year before that." Tyler sank back against the backrest of his chair and ran forked fingers through his hair. "Look, this is likely terrible timing—but then again, it seems like it's time we both took an honest look at the future."

Then Kevin understood. The awful, sinking feeling persisted.

"You don't want my business." That dread had puddled and then cooled.

"I thought it would work. And for a while it did." Tyler's voice quavered. "But the thing is, I drive over an hour and a half to the shop, work eight to ten hours, and then drive an hour and a half home. My wife is pregnant and is trying to make the cupcake shop work. And in the meantime we have two little kids with another on the way. Something's got to give, and the construction job seems like the logical choice. Right now I get home in time to read Evan and Ella a story and then tuck them into bed."

Tyler sat up and settled his gaze on Kevin. "But Evan is going to play T-ball this year, and Ella wants to try dance. If I keep this up, I'll miss it. I'll miss everything, and then I'm going to wake up and they'll be graduating high school, and I'll not know what it was like to see the first time Evan hits a ball or have a memory of kissing my little girl's chubby cheek and telling her to go break a leg at her first recital. And we haven't even touched on the new one coming next year. I don't want to miss these things. I don't want those kinds of regrets."

Tyler sat forward and gripped Kevin's forearm. "I know you worked for over twenty years to build this business. And you did an incredible job. But I can't take it on, Dad. It's not working for my family, and I just can't do it."

There it was. The hard truth. Spoken in love, but difficult to accept nonetheless. Even so, Kevin forced down his own disappointment and looked at the situation from Tyler's perspective—and it was a tough one to be in.

It had been so important to Kevin that he be a dad to his kids. He had desperately wanted his children to have what he'd been denied all his childhood. How could he want less for his grandchildren?

He didn't.

He nodded. "I don't want you to miss those things either."

Tyler exhaled a ragged breath. "Like I said, this timing might be bad. I'm sorry for it."

"What are you thinking, time-wise?"

Propping his elbows on the table, Tyler leaned in. "I'll wrap up the Eisley contract—Brandon is done with his classes and said he'd stay the week after Christmas to help me get it done. Then there are a few bits and pieces to tidy up. By the first of the year . . ."

Less than a month. Kevin's lifework would wrap up in less than a month, and he wouldn't even be able to see it through. He studied the woodgrain of the table while he worked to steady his emotions.

"So that's it then. Retirement is upon me." It sounded utterly pathetic, which Kevin despised. But there it was. He glanced at the leather chair in the corner. "Good thing that's comfortable." More absurd self-pity. Man, was he a grown-up or not?

"Oh no." Tyler knocked on the table with a fist. "Don't you dare do that. I'm not sure who will go nuts first, you or Mom, if you retire yourself to an armchair."

Kevin snorted a small laugh. "That is true. I was just wondering how many *Andy Griffith* reruns I really could handle."

"Watch all you want in the evenings."

With an arched brow, Kevin looked at Ty with a mild challenge. "And during the days?"

Pushing off his elbows, Ty looked down at the table, then smoothed a flat palm over the glossy surface. "This is a nice table, Dad. A really nice piece. Bet it'd sell."

"Your mother would cry."

Tyler shook his head and held a long gaze on him.

Clarity dawned. "Carpentry? Like build furniture?"

"You have the shop already, and it's five minutes away. And this"—he patted the table—"is a reasonable one-man job."

All true. But. "How would I sell them? I don't have a showroom."

"E-commerce, Dad."

"Like I know anything about that."

Tyler winked. "Good thing you have several women in your life who are quite good at it. Not to mention Jacob. He's become an outstanding website designer."

Ah. Yes, that was true. Helen, Lauren, Mackenzie . . . and Ms. Jade Beck, whom he had yet to meet. And Jacob. All were well acquainted with the marketing and selling of goods online.

It had possibilities.

Feeling less pathetic and hopeless, Kevin leaned forward and reached for Tyler's arm. With a pat and then a squeeze, Kevin let the moments settle between them. Both men sipped what remained of their lukewarm coffee.

"What about you?" Kevin asked. "What will you do?"

Tyler crossed his arms. "Matt says he could always use a hand, and Becca could definitely use help in the shop. I usually schedule three or four speaking engagements through the year—maybe I'll add one more." A significant decrease from the twenty a year or so Tyler had done before and shortly after he'd married Becca. He shrugged. "And I'll get to be dad. Like you were."

For all the disappointment that still lingered in knowing that his business was finished and none of his boys would take it over, Kevin clung to that last statement.

He had been a father to his boys. And that had mattered more than any job or business ever could.

CHAPTER EIGHT

(in which there might be a war)

Tyler needed to get to work, but Kevin talked him into a favor before he went.

"You'll not go wandering too far into the park?" Ty asked, brow cocked.

Kevin scowled at him. "I'll wander where I want to, Tyler Murphy, and don't forget that I taught you how to shave and endured your ridiculously bad driving at age sixteen."

"Mom will kill me if something happens to you."

"I had bypass surgery, son. Which means I'm not dead." Shaking his head, though smirking at the banter, Kevin turned to walk toward the gated entrance of the park. "And besides, I get a whole new body on the other side of this life. You all are worrying too much."

"We'd rather not rush that," Ty called, a chuckle in his voice.

Kevin lifted a hand as he strolled down the flagstone path. After a few moments, there came the report of a door shutting on a vehicle and then the sound of Tyler's truck revving its way onto the road.

He would have to call Jacob to come pick him up in about an hour. Hopefully, Helen wouldn't sneak back from her errands by then, because Tyler had only been mildly exaggerating. She would not approve of Kevin slipping off like this unaccompanied.

But some things needed processed on his own.

At the curved fork on the path, Kevin took the right turn—the path less commonly chosen by most. To the left, one would find a park, in the middle of which stood a large gazebo. If he chose to inspect that structure closely, a fellow would come across a gold plate engraved with *Murphy Builds, 1995.*

It had been one of his first contracts, and he'd been thrilled. But that memory was not what had prompted him to visit the Sugar Pine open space.

The right-hand path came with a bit of an incline. Strange, he'd not noticed that detail on any of his other visits.

Breath puffing heavily and white before his face, and a bit lightheaded, Kevin paused at the bend in the way, which was also at the crest of that incline, and gazed at the familiar view.

Headstones poked up from the thin layer of snow on the ground, each one straight and tidy. Each one bearing the name that mattered to somebody somewhere. To Kevin, there were three in this cemetery that he visited.

Stride slow, he made his way to the first—the one that had stood in its assigned place the longest.

David Matthew Clayton 1962–1996. Son. Friend. Good and faithful servant.

Kevin's brows pinched as the old ache resurfaced. Not as it once did—not with the roiling anger at the man who had taken his best friend's life, at the unfairness of it. No, in fact, following George's lead—one Kevin had a hard time wrapping his mind around—Kevin had met Aaron Knipp. Had gotten to know him as he met with him at AA meetings after Aaron had finished his jail time. And ultimately had forgiven the man. Which he well should—and it maybe shouldn't have been so hard. After all, Kevin had been in a drunk-driving accident as well. It could have just as easily been him in Aaron's shoes.

But a mild ache was still there. Kevin missed this friend who had become a brother to him. He also still felt deeply for George and Elizabeth.

As if on autopilot, Kevin's feet moved, taking him to the next headstone.

George William Clayton. 1936–2008. Honored, loved, and greatly missed.

That one had also come as an unexpected blow. One night George and Elizabeth were over at the Murphys', engaged in a lively game of dominos, and the next day Kevin had received a call from Elizabeth. George had suffered a massive heart attack. The hospital had declared him dead on arrival.

Elizabeth took it with the sort of strength and courage that made Kevin stand in awe. Some days he still couldn't comprehend it.

Brushing the cold, smooth top of George's headstone, he turned a forty-five-degree angle to his left and wandered four rows across, three more back.

This marker was newer, though the dirt had settled. Beneath the snow, waiting for spring's warmer temperatures, the grass had filled in thick. And this one coiled the most pain around his heart. Because the ache was closer in time, and it had pierced him as a father. That was a unique sort of pain—something Kevin could have gone without knowing.

Sadie Allen Murphy.

One of his own. Not of his body, but by a son. A daughter-in-love who bore his name and had claimed a spot of her own in his heart. A sweet, strong young woman who had made Connor happy and had given them Reid.

Heaven knew, Kevin had tried to surrender to God on this. But heaven knew, that hadn't gone well. Because Connor had done the right thing—a noble thing. And because it seemed like a tease to have Sadie get well, declared cancer free, only to die of it a few years later.

And because it was helpless agony to watch your child go through that sort of deep grief.

There had been so many unanswered whys. So many sleepless nights full of spiritual wrestling matches with God.

And there had been the terribly hard thing of witnessing Samuel and Eleanor Allen as they'd walked through the same grief, only certainly deeper, darker. Because Sadie was *their* daughter. Like George and Elizabeth, they'd only had one child, and they'd buried her.

How did one reconcile God's goodness with that?

Kevin hated it, but the truth was, some days there was simply defeat. There was doubt. He would yell at God in anger and frustration. And then weep because it didn't help. It didn't change anything.

What it did do was summon the question as old as the book of Job—why do bad things happen to good people?

Why do God's people go through hard stuff?

I wish I could understand.

Kevin squeezed his eyes shut as that decades-old conversation resurfaced. He'd had it with George several months after Dave died. At the point when George had started meeting with the man who had killed his own son.

That had seemed too much to ask.

George had looked at a younger Kevin when he'd muttered that very sentiment. His eyes held sorrow but also warning. *My boy, what if it had been you?*

Indeed, what if? Kevin didn't think he could live with himself if he'd been that driver. But he well could have been.

Anger, shame, and frustration had clutched him in a hard, tangled-up ball. *Why would God let that happen though? Why would he let this happen to Dave? To you? I keep trying to make it make sense, but it doesn't, and that scares me.*

George had nodded, no censure in his eyes, and gripped Kevin's forearm. *I know.*

Of course George knew. Dave had been *his* son. He should be the one angry and upset in this conversation, not the one holding steady, consoling.

I wish I could understand. Why do bad things happen . . . He didn't finish the murky question.

To good people?

Kevin nodded.

I've been thinking that too. Asking it.

And?

No answer, Kevin. I don't have an answer. But I've been struck with another question lately.

What's that?

What if God is showing the heavenlies that there are faithful men? People who will choose to say, "Yet shall I praise you," even when it hurts and it's not fair and it doesn't make sense?

Why would He need to do that?

Because there is a war, Kevin, and we are in the middle of it. Satan says that people will only be as faithful as far as the blessings go. God has claimed that there are some who will be faithful beyond that. People who will love Him no matter what comes.

Their conversation had gone on for quite some time. Kevin had argued that he didn't want to be part of a cosmic bet. If there was a war, he wanted out of the middle of it.

George had calmly, humbly responded that perhaps that wasn't up to them.

It had been a profound conversation. One that Kevin had wrestled with on and off through the years. And was the real reason he'd wanted to visit the cemetery today, after Tyler made his announcement.

Once again Kevin found himself in a circumstance he didn't anticipate and certainly hadn't wanted. Letting go of Murphy Builds was hard—so much harder than he'd imagined. Mostly because he hadn't imagined that his business wouldn't survive his retirement. He'd intended it to be a legacy to pass on to his sons. Maybe even his grandchildren.

Today, that dream ended.

It wasn't the same awful pain that Kevin had known losing these people that he'd loved. But it was pretty dang hard.

But there had been this wonderful, faithful man named George who had taught Kevin to seek a heavenly perspective in hard places. To change his age-old, unknowable question of *why this?* to instead *will I be faithful?* And then to pray that God would make him so.

With the few minutes he had left before he needed to call Jacob for a ride, Kevin knelt in the wet snow and proceeded with that prayer.

Helen rubbed her arms as she paced the kitchen, telling herself everything was fine.

Trust the Lord. And your husband . . .

Except, that was a bit of a challenge right then, since she couldn't find Kevin and he wasn't answering his phone. Why had he snuck off? Couldn't he have at least left a note so she'd know if she needed to go tromping through the snow to help him?

Lord! Where is he?

She hadn't felt this panicked about Kevin in years. Not since he'd quit drinking.

The sound of footfalls echoing on the front deck steps made her stop in her tracks and pivot to face the front door.

Stomp. Stomp. Stomp.

A familiar routine—Kevin always made sure he didn't track in snow. Helen held her breath, hope and expectation pounding in her chest while a sudden wave of irritation built deep in her gut.

The door opened, and there he stood. Stocking cap covering his salt-and-pepper hair, dark shadow of his evening beard on his jaw. Relief at the sight of him had Helen scurrying.

"Kevin!" Flinging herself against him was an overreaction and likely not wise, considering what he'd been through the past few weeks, but Helen did so anyway.

His coat was cold against her, but she clung to him just the same. "Where have you been?"

Arms that had held her since she'd been eighteen years old wrapped her close. "To visit the three."

That rise of irritation threatened to breach her mouth, but she tamped it down. Visiting the three was a solemn practice for her husband. And by the way he curled around her and laid his head atop hers, there was emotion weighing against his heart.

"I was worried," she whispered.

He cradled her head with one hand. "I'm sorry. I thought I'd be out and back before you were done in town."

"Sneaking around?" She tilted her head back, and he moved so that she could look into his eyes. "That's not good."

The pads of his fingers were chilled as he traced the outline of her face with them. But at his gentle touch, she closed her eyes.

"Let's not live in fear, Helen. We left that behind a long time ago. Let's not go backward."

She opened her eyes to find his tender gaze caressing her. "But you almost died."

"Almost. Not yet."

"I need to know you're okay."

A faint, crooked grin lifted one corner of his mouth. "I'm here. But, my sweet, semi-control-freak wife, you can't wrap me up and put me in your pocket. We'll both go crazy."

He was right, and she'd known so before the words were spoken. They'd had such similar conversations about their boys over the years. She wanted to know they were safe and happy and doing well all the time. What mother wouldn't?

But this constant worry . . . led to fussing, and that almost always led nowhere good. Jackson and Jacob were her prime examples.

Put your hope in God, maker of heaven and earth.

Silently, while her husband tucked her against him and indulged her with a long embrace, Helen surrendered her anxious heart again. Seemed she would have to over and over for the rest of her life.

Sighing, Helen rubbed Kevin's back and then stepped out of the shelter of his arms so that he could take off his winter coat and hat and come in past the entry.

"Do you want some tea?" she asked, going to her electric teakettle.

"No." Kevin's voice was firm, but gentle. "I don't want any more tea, Helen. I would take a cup of coffee though."

She looked at him, and their gazes locked. With that same gentle, cock-eyed grin on his handsome face, Kevin closed the space between them, and his hand took hers. "Decaf."

Ah, the charm of Kevin Murphy. Before Helen could fight it back, her own grin slipped onto her mouth. "Decaf?"

"My compromise. For now."

With an exaggerated sigh, Helen relented. "All right, then."

He lifted her hand and pressed a kiss to her knuckles and then released her as she turned back to the counter. Within five minutes they both had their warm mugs—his full of decaf coffee, and hers of peach tea—and Helen followed him to the couch.

"Why did you go to the cemetery today?" Helen adjusted her seat so that she faced him.

"I needed perspective. I don't know why I find it best there—maybe that's morbid. But I do." Kevin leaned to place his mug on the coffee table and then turned toward her. "Ty doesn't want the business."

Helen's heart sank, though she wasn't shocked. Honestly, she'd wondered how long Tyler would continue commuting to work for his dad. It wasn't a great setup for a man with a family.

Even so, she'd never brought up her concerns. Kevin had worked so hard to make Murphy Builds the thriving enterprise it was. And he'd dreamed of leaving it to their boys someday.

Leaning close, Helen slid her palm against the rough plane of his jaw. "I'm sorry, hon."

His Adam's apple bobbed as he swallowed. "I should have seen it. Poor kid had to sit there and tell me he needed to be done, and that couldn't have been easy. But . . ."

"But it means letting it go."

Lips pressed tight, he nodded.

Helen curved her hand around his head, her fingers burrowing into his thick hair, and she drew his head toward hers.

For several quiet moments he stayed stiff and still, and then he drew her back against him. She could feel the shuddering of his breath as he exhaled. "I just needed to lay down all the whys again."

The perennial human battle, it seemed. Helen had more of her own than she could count. Sometimes faith was really hard.

But if they remembered how God had been faithful in the past, it might make this test easier.

CHAPTER NINE

(in which flowers have meaning)

T wo solid weeks.

Helen exhaled the relief that marker brought. Kevin had been out of the hospital, through the first few days of rehab, and home now for a full two weeks. That marked just over three weeks since the event that had turned their world upside down.

With Chopin playing softly in the background, she laid out the separated stem varieties that had been stored in buckets of water in her workroom. Fir boughs for structure, arborvitae stems for soft texture, red dogwood stems for variety and a shot of color, and white hypericum for contrast berries. As she arranged the piles of stems on her worktable so that making her bundles would be as simple as walking down the line, Helen hummed the notes of *Nocturne in C-Sharp Minor*.

"How can I help?" Kenzie walked through the French double doors that separated the main house from this sunroom addition Kevin had built for Helen's work space. Had that been thirteen years ago? She still felt spoiled by it.

With a grateful smile, Helen looked up at her daughter-in-love, now of ten years. Goodness those years had made such a difference in Kenzie. When she'd first stepped into the Murphys' home, newly married to Jackson but a stranger to everyone else in the family, Helen had been uncertain.

Why had Jackson married a woman no one had ever heard of before, she'd wondered. And Kenzie had been so reserved. So very much *unlike*

Jackson, the wild prankster who loved a boisterous laugh more than anything else. But at that time, Helen already had one estranged son and daughter-in-law. She certainly did not want to risk that again. So she'd put on a bright face and welcomed Kenzie into their family, no questions asked.

Oh-ho-ho! If she'd known the real backstory on Jackson and Kenzie, she might well have behaved differently. Praise God she *hadn't* known. And praise God He'd worked in both Jackson's and Kenzie's lives in a powerful way—using sweet little Bobbie Joy in the process.

My thoughts are not your thoughts, nor are my ways your ways . . . The verse from Jeremiah whispered through Helen's mind as she collected the stems for her first bundle. This was a season to remember God's faithfulness.

Nodding to the plant material, she answered Kenzie. "You know the drill, flower girl. Though you're not obligated to help."

Having done arrangements and bouquets for ten years alongside Helen, Kenzie filed easily in line. "Jackson took the kids out to the Storm Café for ice cream. I get a grown-up time-out, and this is the perfect way to spend it."

Chuckling, a passing wonder drifted through Helen's mind about what Kenzie's mother thought of her daughter mothering *four* children. She prayed those sweet kids were used by God to make an impression on the cold woman's closed heart.

Helen finished her first bundle with a decorative pick of felt gingerbread men pulled through the middle. With a few bits of rearranging, she examined the fistful of green in her hand and, satisfied, took it over to the stem cutter anchored at the end of her wooden table. With a quick hard cut, she trimmed the stems and then wrapped the base with a thick rubber band. Finally, she slid the bundle into a paper sleeve and placed the final product in a waiting bucket of fresh water.

One down, twenty-four more to go.

"You know, Jackson thinks you should have canceled this order." Kenzie lined up her gathered bundle with the stem cutter.

After the sharp *whack!* of the blade sounded, Helen met Kenzie's gaze. "I didn't want to." Every one of her boys had suggested that very thing. No, not *suggested*. Very nearly demanded.

Men.

Then again, she'd been overbearing to Kevin, so perhaps that was just desserts.

Helen shook her head and rolled her eyes. "As I informed Matthew last night, when he tried to bully me out of helping Lauren with the two-foot trees later today, I am not a wimp. Not some fragile doll they need to put in a glass cabinet. I'm doing fine—and so is Dad." Kevin had reminded her so just the evening before.

Kenzie chuckled softly. "I think sometimes they forget that you raised seven boys."

"Exactly." Helen started on the next bundle. "Seven rambunctious, ever-hungry, and always-into-everything boys. What do they think I would do with my time anyway? Sit and stare at Kevin? He would absolutely *not* appreciate that."

"That would be . . . weird."

"Very. And as handsome as he is, quite boring. And as I mentioned, he'd get annoyed. He's already irritated that he can't drive nails and cut boards with Tyler, and just last night he insisted I let him have coffee. Decaf—that was the deal."

"Uh-ho. Is he getting antsy?"

"Antsy and, frankly, a little grumpy." Helen winked. "But I called the doctor today, and he's cleared to go for a twenty-minute walk every day. We'll start this evening."

One after the other, they both chopped the stems and wrapped their bundles, and then, as if on autopilot, started on the next pair. They did the next set in silence, and then Kenzie spoke again.

"I'm glad I get to see these things," she said.

"What things?"

"The everyday things with you and Kevin. That way, when I get annoyed with Jackson because he so over the top most of the time, I can rest assured that it's normal and we'll be okay."

"Jackson? Annoying?" Helen snorted. "I cannot imagine my sweet baby boy is ever annoying."

Chuckling at Helen's sarcasm, Kenzie nodded. "But in all seriousness, if I didn't see you and Kevin sometimes go crossways and recover, I wouldn't know that it was okay. To this day my mom swears marriage is a trap and could never really work in a way that a woman could be happy. It's good to see that's not true."

Pausing after she placed a new bundle in the bucket, Helen reached for Kenzie's arm. "And are you happy?"

The smile on her face was all the tell needed. "You raised a good one, Mama Helen. Seven of them, I think."

Hadn't been just her raising those boys, and she and Kevin certainly hadn't done it perfectly. There had been many times over the years, in fact, that they'd desperately prayed for crop failure when it came to things they'd sown into their children.

Kevin's alcoholism from their early years. Her propensity to worry and be a control freak. Just two of many examples.

Kenzie turned to begin another bouquet bundle. "This year is forty for you two, right?"

"It is." Plucking up a bough of fir, Helen paused to inhale the fresh fragrance of clean forest. It smelled nothing like the bouquet she'd carried forty years ago—a small bundle of leather leaf green, baby's breath, and three red roses that Kevin had purchased, likely at a grocery store, the day before their wedding.

She shook her head and breathed out a tiny laugh.

"What's funny?" Kenzie asked.

"I was remembering the flowers I carried for our wedding. Kevin got them for me—otherwise I wasn't going to have any flowers."

"You? Not have flowers at your wedding?"

"I know, crazy, right? And it had made me so sad, because even back then I loved flowers. But all the money for the wedding went basically to my ridiculously lacey and poofy dress. After that the tiered cake that was all important in an eighties wedding. So no money for flowers. At the rehearsal, I was acting off, and Kevin asked what was wrong. I told him I didn't have a bouquet—which wasn't entirely the whole truth of what was actually wrong. He ran to the store in between rehearsal and dinner and bought me flowers."

"What was actually wrong?"

Having just cut stems on another bouquet, Helen paused and looked at Kenzie. "I was scared to death."

A thoughtful, and perhaps somewhat surprised look, passed over Kenzie's expression, and it occurred to Helen that though it had been a decade since Kenzie had married Jackson, perhaps Mackenzie didn't know the whole story of Kevin and Helen Murphy. Did any of her sons' wives?

Certainly the boys did, didn't they? It wasn't like Helen and Kevin had kept it a secret from them. But it also wasn't something that they spoke about often.

"You were nervous about the wedding or about getting married?"

Helen finished wrapping the bouquet and then gave Kenzie her full attention. "I was pregnant, Kenz."

Lips parted, Kenzie's brows lifted. "You were . . . oh." Rose colored her cheeks. "I didn't know . . ."

"You aren't the only one—though I'm sorry if it seems like we hid this from you. We didn't—not intentionally. I'm sure the boys all know our story. I think." Helen paused, biting her lip. "Anyway, I was nearly a month pregnant with Matt when we got married. It was a rushed thing, and we were both very young. I was quite frankly terrified out of my mind."

"Did your parents force you to marry?"

"Oh no. They weren't in favor of it at all. They didn't like Kevin."

"You're kidding me."

"No, I'm not. And I don't think Kevin would mind me telling you that they had good reason to *not* like him. He drank back then. A lot."

Kenzie blinked. Clearly she'd known nothing about this. Hadn't they told the boys? Maybe some of them, but perhaps not all? With seven children, it'd be easy to neglect certain things—especially in the middle of the chaotic business of living.

But they hadn't intended to hide their past. Honestly.

"I'm sorry, Helen." Kenzie simply stared at her in shock. "I am just trying to imagine this. I can't picture it. You and Kevin have always been so . . . so steady. Happy. Such good Christian people."

"Not always, sweet girl. Not even close to always." Helen gripped Kenzie's hand and drew her to the deep windowsill where they could sit. "And I thought Jackson knew our past. I'm sorry if this seems like we've been lying to you. It wasn't intentional."

"Perhaps he does and it's just never come up." Kenzie shrugged. "Anyway, I doubt it would make a difference to him. Or to me, really."

"Hmm." Helen looked over her shoulder out the window and into the late-afternoon sky. Scattered clouds dotted the light-blue canvas, but nothing that should prevent the evening walk Kevin wanted.

Glad of it, she turned her attention back to Kenzie. "Just to clear the air, let me just tell you all of it. I wanted, more than anything, to have a storybook romance. I wanted the fairy tale that back then it had seemed

Princess Dianna had. I wanted my very own prince to swoop into my life and change it. Make it special and lovely. And into that longing of an eighteen-year-old girl swooped a twenty-year-old guy who desperately longed for his life to matter to someone. So there we were, two broken, empty people hoping the other could fill the void."

"That sounds like the beginnings to a not-good end."

"Exactly so." Helen pressed her lips together as she remembered the hopelessness that had marked her days long after her marriage. How it had seemed such a massive mistake, but there had been no way out. There had been crushing disappointment in it, but also so much brokenheart-edness—because even in her ignorant youth, she had loved the man she'd married. And he'd loved her. But they couldn't seem to figure out how to make each other happy. How to be whole together.

"But for the grace of God." Helen borrowed the old Bradford quote as she squeezed Kenzie's hand. "Life could have easily looked so much differently than it does now."

With a gentle smile of understanding—that from her own story of grace and salvation—Kenzie nodded and followed Helen back to the table so they could finish the last of the bouquets.

"What would you have rather carried for your wedding?" Kenzie asked.

Caught off guard, Helen sent her a quizzical look.

"I mean for your wedding bouquet," the younger woman clarified. "Now that you're a professional with flowers, what would you have chosen?"

Seemed such an odd and random question. Then again, Kenzie had adopted Helen's love for all things floral, so perhaps it was a natural curiosity. Helen paused, midmotion of tucking in a stem of hypericum.

"Well, they wouldn't be very seasonal for a Christmastime wedding, but I think if I could pick anything, I would want a whole fistful of snowdrops and Mount Hood Daffodils."

A full smile spread on Kenzie's face, causing her coppery eyes to dance. Helen thought, as she had many times over, that Jackson must have fallen in love with those lovely eyes and the smattering of sweet freckles long before he'd known this girl's name.

"Flowers of hope and perseverance." Kenzie dipped an approving nod. "Entirely perfect, I'd say."

CHAPTER TEN

(in which old debts demand a high price)

K evin savored the hand in his. For forty years this woman had walked beside him, offered the silent comfort of her presence, lent him the strength and determination to make a better life.

Thank God for Helen Chase Murphy.

As he inhaled the crisp evening air, a breath full of sharp pine, Kevin did exactly that.

This path was not one they took often. Usually when going out for a walk—or rather in this terrain, a miniature hike—they opted to take the hillside trail to the lookout. But that late afternoon, after slipping into coats and donning stocking caps, he and Helen set their direction on an older trail that had become nearly indiscernible over the years.

Because it led to a place Kevin didn't like to think on often. He didn't hike that way, and when it was used, it was accessed by the poorly maintained four-wheel-drive road.

That afternoon, however, he felt called to walk that direction. Though she glanced at him with a questioning look when he pulled back a bough that had grown over the trail entrance, Helen didn't voice her query. Instead, her hand securely in his, she followed his path as it led deeper into a new-growth forest.

They had planted many of the sugar pines and white spruces that now reached above their heads, in an effort to restore the forest that had wilted to beetle damage. Clearing the dead and replanting the new had been grueling work, but it had been important to them—and a means of small income for their sons over the years.

To Kevin, this bit of forest was symbolic of his life. The felling of the old, the diseased, the toxic. Such hard and often painful work. But necessary. And then the planting of the new. Sometimes those seedlings didn't make it. There was the frustration and loss of money, time, and effort, yet the determination to try again. To keep at it.

By the passage of time, the persistence of effort, and ultimately, the grace of God, they walked through a healthy stand of trees. Hand in hand, now sharing a healthy and beautiful life.

Their trail spilled into a small clearing. On the far side stood the place Kevin didn't like to visit. The shack that had been his childhood home.

It didn't look like a shack anymore. Hadn't for quite some time. They'd used it every now and then. For overflow of guests. Even as a home for Brandon for a few years, before he'd fallen in love with his arranged fiancée and shocked everyone by actually marrying her.

It had also served as five of his sons' childhood home for a few years. And that was why he was there.

Five feet into the clearing, and with an unhindered view of that tiny house, Kevin stopped and let the emotion of so many memories overtake him. Silently, as if knowing why they were there, Helen released his hand and slipped her arm around his, offering him the strength of her presence.

"I really, really didn't want us to live there," Kevin said in a low voice.

She pressed her head into his shoulder. "I know."

"How long do you intend to have my daughter work herself ragged to pay your debts?"

Jim Chase's words hit like fiery arrows against Kevin's heart. It had taken years for Mr. Chase to even speak to Helen again. He'd been so terribly angry that they'd lied to him. Kevin believed his father-in-law hated him for getting his eighteen-year-old daughter pregnant and then covering it up by jumping into a rushed and unapproved marriage. Connor had been a baby before the man chose to acknowledge that he had any grandsons, let alone three.

Now, nearly four, as Helen was expecting. Again.

Alongside that piercing shame his father-in-law had just fired into Kevin's heart came a familiar thrashing panic. How was he supposed to be a father to *four* children? He'd been sober for almost two years, and with each passing day he saw his own insufficiencies with more clarity.

Kevin loved his sons. And he loved his wife. He loved having a family. But he had no better idea of how to be the kind of husband and father he wanted to be than when he'd married Helen five years before. All he had was a desperate thirst to do better and a hope that his mornings spent with God in His Word and weekly meetings with George and Dave would aid the transformation he longed for.

And countless prayers that usually went something like, *By Your Spirit, Lord, make me the man you would have me to be.*

"I don't want her to work the night shifts at the diner."

Kevin had never liked that Helen had taken that job, but he couldn't argue with her when she'd showed him that they needed the money to pay off hospital bills. "But we can't figure out another way—"

Mr. Chase scowled at him. "Sure seems stupid for a man to keep making babies when he can't take care of his family."

Gut clenching hard, Kevin thought he might puke. He couldn't argue that point. Rolling his fists, he could only stare at his shoes while heat burned his neck and face.

His own father's comments came steamrolling into his memory from four years past, before his dad had died. After Matt's birth, Dad had come to see his grandchild. The man was semi-sober at best, stumbling into the trailer house smelling like cheap vodka and week-old man sweat. After peeking over the bassinet, little more than an impassive nod to acknowledge the baby, he began counting months on his fingers.

He stopped at eight and shook his head. "Knocked her up before you married her, didn't you, boy?"

Kevin couldn't form an answer and begged whoever might be in charge of the planet, if there was such a being, that Helen hadn't overheard from their bedroom.

"Becoming more and more like your old man every day. Hopefully, she won't stick you with him." With that, his dad had left.

Man, he'd come from bad stock.

Two perfectly horrible moments, spread apart by years but blended by the same scathing sensation of disdain and utter hopelessness. If Kevin had still been a drinking man, he might have followed his dad's path to the grave that night after Helen's parents had left. Instead, he sat in a chair, alone in the dark while his three sons slept and Helen waited tables at a truck-stop diner.

Hands pressed hard against his temple, Kevin couldn't stop the seeping of hot tears. "God, help."

Into the misery of his self-loathing there came an image of the shack. Kevin pressed the heels of his palms against his eyes and tried to will it away.

He hated his childhood home. It was tiny and dark and stank of liquor, vomit, and human filth. It held memories of him hiding under his bed from his embarrassingly drunk father, and the ironic fear that would electrify his veins when he would find the man passed out on the floor the next day.

What if that was the day that he found his dad dead? He would be alone in the world. What would happen to him then? Though Kevin had lived with sharp humiliation at having the town drunk for a father, he couldn't imagine what would happen to him if his dad died.

Even as a grown man, one who was saved and seeking to live as God would have him to—now free from his father's legacy of drunkenness—Kevin felt the thundering panic and smothering shame of those long-ago memories. How could he ever think to go back to the crappy house that contained every horrible moment of his life?

But that shack belonged to him now. Left to him along with twenty-five acres, by some strange twist of fate Kevin could not comprehend, by his worthless dad who had died shortly after Jacob had been born.

Seemed his father's death should have been a relief, and to a measure it was. But the loathing Kevin had for the man didn't die with the man himself. Nor did the fear, shame, and loneliness that stupid little house provoked. For much of the time since his father's death, Kevin had said he didn't want to look into that inheritance, because heaven knew what he'd find. Likely a debt of back taxes or something that would only drag him and Helen further into the pit.

But try as he might to push away the image of a place that haunted him, Kevin knew it had been pressed into his mind for a reason. By the One he'd just cried to for help.

Because there wasn't a debt of back taxes on the property. Another mystery he couldn't work out but knew now for a fact after the county had told him a year ago that he needed to do something with the place. His father had passed the property to Kevin free and clear.

A man can only have property. And if he has that, he has everything.

Words pressed into a vague memory somewhere around Kevin's tenth year. He couldn't remember why his dad had said it, but the voice carrying the words was his father's. Apparently, that land was the only thing the man had truly valued in his entire life.

And he'd left it to Kevin.

The solution lay in front of him. But that required Kevin to face the ghosts that lay in his past. He hadn't been sure that he could.

Helen had been exhausted when she'd come home from her shift. Seven months pregnant with baby number four, a full four hours on her feet had taxed her to a breaking point. Her legs ached, ankles swollen and hot. Her back spasmed at intervals, and all she wanted was to fall into bed and let sleep claim her.

Though it was after ten, Kevin was still awake when she slid gratefully between the sheets beside him. He rolled toward her, kissed her forehead, and reached to flick on the lamp on her side of the bed.

"Hi," she murmured sleepily.

His gentle kiss found her lips. "Hi, babe." His pause felt somehow disappointed. "You're tired."

"Hmm." Helen pushed her fingers into his hair. "Very."

Silence stretched between them as Kevin remained hovering over her. Helen felt his study behind her closed eyes. "You okay?"

"Not really."

At his starkly honest answer, her eyes fluttered open. Once again she reached to finger his hair, this time at his forehead. "What's wrong?"

"I think we need to move . . ." His swallow bobbed at his neck, and hesitant emotion passed through his intense gaze. "Move into the cabin."

"The cabin?" He couldn't mean what she thought. It simply wasn't within him. Sure, she'd thought of it—the fact that there wouldn't be any rent. No plot dues. It would mean speeding up paying off his hospital bills from two years past, not to mention the fees for this next baby. If everything was only a financial decision, moving into his childhood home—the place his dad had left for him—made sense.

But everything was *not* about money. The last thing Helen wanted for her husband—a man who was growing more and more into someone respectable, someone she'd once only hoped he could be—was for him to be tossed back into the emotional chaos of his childhood.

For Kevin, that cabin was haunted. She would work the late shift every night for the rest of her life to spare him that.

"It makes sense." His voice held both reserve and resolve, though Helen wasn't sure how that was possible.

"No it doesn't."

"Yes, my love, it does. It's paid for."

"It's not really livable," she countered. And that was somewhat true. It would take money to make it a place that their growing family could set up home in—and even then it'd be cramped. Not exactly moving up in the world, as there would be no more space than this little trailer house provided.

"Most of that is superficial. I can fix it." Kevin's palm covered the baby growing in her belly.

Helen placed her hand over his. "Kevin, we're okay here."

"No, we're not." Emotion caught in his voice. "I don't want you working yourself ragged anymore. I don't want you to pay for my stupidity like this. It's . . ." He drew in a shuddering inhale. "It's humiliating, Helen."

"Kevin," she whispered, tears hot in her eyes.

"It is, and I don't want things to be this way anymore. I would rather face everything that I've been running from than to see you exhausted all the time. I would rather my sons grow up knowing I was brave enough to deal with the things in my past, rather than them finding out that you worked the way you do because I was too much of a coward to handle it." His hand slid from her womb, and then he was cupping her face. "I would rather be able to look your dad in the eye."

"My dad?"

Lips pursed, his eyes slid shut, and he nodded.

"What about my dad?"

Silence was his extended answer.

"Kevin, whatever my dad did or said doesn't matt—"

"Yes it does, Helen. It matters a great deal. When it comes to you, I have been nothing but sneaky, disrespectful, and dishonorable to him. How can that possibly show him Christ in me? How can we by any measure be a testimony to him, the way you want to be, if I remain that sort of man?"

"You're not. You're sober now."

"It's not enough."

"It's everything."

He shook his head. "No. Not for him. Not for me." Lips pressed tight again, Kevin couldn't continue, but his thick emotion bled through his gaze.

Helen fingered one dark, thick eyebrow. "You work so hard. We'll get it paid off."

"I'll continue to work hard." Kevin gathered her in close. "But I think this is what we should do. We can pay off my bill before this baby comes."

She felt his pensiveness about it. It didn't matter who understood or didn't, Helen knew the cost this move would require of her husband's heart. She knew his fear of it. It made her own anxiety about moving into the place of his bad memories heighten.

Into that unease, Helen knew an anger directed at her dad. Whatever he had said and done—and it was clear that Kevin wasn't going to share that bit with her—it wasn't needed. She didn't think it was helpful, and in her heart there arose a powerful defender longing to shield her husband from her dad's censure.

If her dad only knew the shadows that lurked in Kevin's childhood. If he really understood the difficulties Kevin faced now . . . perhaps he wouldn't push her husband to such hard measures.

But Helen also sensed Kevin's need for this.

She'd seen the dimness in his eyes every time she got ready to go to the diner. The way his broad shoulders would curve inward, the way his gaze would cast toward the floor when she kissed him good night before she left for her shift. When she would share with him how much she'd made in tips on a good night—every cent earmarked to pay off the hospital bill—he would nod silently and swallow. She'd witnessed his fight for gratitude in the midst of the shame.

That wasn't what she wanted for him either.

In the shelter of his arms, Helen shut her eyes and prayed. *Lord, is this Your way for us? Because it scares me. I don't want to lose him . . .*

That was her greatest fear—that she would lose the husband she loved more every day to the powerful grip of a bottle. Driven back to it by the memories and emotions that still dredged his heart. And if she did lose him, it seemed certain that it would be for forever this time.

The idea of it shredded her heart.

This move would take every bit as much faith from her as it would from Kevin. Even then Helen wasn't certain it would be enough.

CHAPTER ELEVEN

(in which blessings must be acknowledged)

K evin pointed across the meadow in front of them, up the hill to the south of the little cabin. Silently, Helen nodded at his side, and then they trekked toward the spot.

There wasn't a marker. Nothing ceremoniously placed to remember. But he remembered nonetheless. At the base of a trio of fir, he had scattered his father's ashes.

Helen slipped her hand back into his, and when they stopped several feet from those trees, her fingers squeezed. "You've been thinking about him?"

Nodding, Kevin rubbed his chin. "A lot. Especially while I was in the hospital."

Sliding her hand from his, she wrapped his waist with her arm. "I've been thinking about the past so much lately too." Tipping her chin up, she met his gaze. "Why your dad though?"

Kevin turned into her embrace and pulled her in close. "I think because of my struggle with Sadie's death." It didn't make sense, not on the surface. But even though he was certain his wife didn't follow his thoughts, she remained steady against him, willing to let him process. He curled around her warm frame, savoring the safety he always felt with her in his arms. "There's still bitterness in me, Helen, and it cracked open when we had to watch Connor and Sadie go through that. When I had to watch our son writhe with that kind of pain, it spilled out the leftover bitterness I've kept all these years."

"At God?"

He had thought and prayed over that possibility long and hard. The conviction of it wasn't there—that wasn't the source. Kevin shook his head. "No. Strangely, no." He stepped back from her and faced the trees again. "The bitterness is still toward my dad."

"I wouldn't have guessed that. I never saw it in you, Kevin."

It would have been easy to hide. Kevin rarely mentioned his dad. Rarely thought of him. The few times the man had ever come up, it was in reference to drinking—and that as a warning to his faltering sons. First Jackson, who had wandered into a bottle for a time after high school.

Your grandfather was an alcoholic, son. He literally drank himself to death. Is that the path you want to wander down?

It had seemed that was enough to ward Jackson off. At least at the time, as a few years later Jackson showed up with Kenzie, his new wife. The one who later, Jackson confessed, he'd married in Vegas when they'd both been too hammered to know what they were doing.

God, that story could have gone so differently. So badly.

As He had been with Kevin, God had been astonishingly merciful. Kevin couldn't help but worship His goodness when he thought on Jackson and Kenzie's healthy, loving marriage—a beautiful picture of redemption.

As good as those thoughts were, though, that wasn't what he was dealing with that day. Today was about bitterness he'd allowed to linger far too long. Kevin had tried to bury the murky emotions he still owned toward his dad. But they refused to stay pushed into the depths.

Perhaps because in his dad's story, Kevin saw no redemption.

There was such an emptiness to that. It was the same gaping space that Kevin felt as he had watched Sadie get sicker and sicker, as he had wrestled with the stark reality that this time, she would not recover. The same hollowness that he felt when he'd helplessly witnessed his son and grandson at her funeral, and the many months that followed. That void filled with ache, and, though he hadn't wanted to admit it, with the bitterness he hadn't owned or dealt with.

Bitterness at his dad's unrepentant life. The unredeemed story. At the legacy his dad had pressed into Kevin—one that had nearly destroyed not only Kevin's own life but that of Helen's and their three older sons.

Staring at the forest floor where he had spread his dad's ashes, Kevin swallowed and braced himself for confession. "For all these years, my dad has been this shadow lurking in the past. A man unredeemed. A man who would always stand as a threat to the life that we have now. The life that I have loved." A tear flicked from one eye onto his cheek. He looked down at his wife, who stood with eyes shimmering, full of love and deep empathy. To say what was at the heart of his struggle was hard. But this woman had seen the worst of him more than once over the years, and she had chosen love.

She would that day as well. Kevin had no doubt.

He gathered the scraps of determination and courage he needed to finish. His words came out harsh, broken with the force of long-kept emotion. "I have never forgiven him for it."

Helen's lips trembled, and she blinked. The bleeding of his heart most certainly felt keenly in hers. With her free hand, she gently covered his chest, wary of the point of incision where the surgeon had gone in to bypass the blocked artery that had nearly killed him.

An appropriate picture of this bitterness problem if ever there was one. Although Kevin didn't want a bypass on his spiritual heart. He wanted full healing. There was only One to whom he knew to turn for it.

He put honest courage to it again. Shutting his eyes, he tilted his face toward the heavens. "God . . . forgive me. For all the years of stored bitterness. Forgive me. For the secret corner of doubt I've kept in my heart—the one that has questioned Your goodness. Forgive me. And for not choosing gratitude over anger when I think on my father. Forgive me."

That last one, it might have been the hardest. In his anger and resentment toward his dad, he had maintained that there was nothing to be grateful for—except perhaps for the narrow escape from the man's legacy of addiction.

Kevin looked back down at Helen, feeling that the truth needed to be spoken out loud. That way he would be less prone to forget it.

"This place . . . it was so hard to move into." He glanced back at the cabin. They'd lived in it for a little more than three years. Three years of not paying rent because the land and the cabin were owned. Kevin had no idea what a big deal that would become just a few short months after they'd moved in. For in that time, Jackson had been born. Another baby boy who looked mostly like Kevin, with thick dark hair and nut-brown eyes.

And a cleft palate.

The medical bills could have buried them. But they didn't.

"I never said what a blessing it was." Kevin turned to Helen, taking both her hands in his. "The truth is, my dad left me something amazing. For all of his faults, all the things I hated and resented, somehow he held on to this property, and he left it to me. More than once it changed how we could live. It provided in a way that I never could have otherwise. But up until this moment, I wasn't thankful to my dad for it. Because I didn't want to give him credit for anything good."

Helen's tender gaze never flickered into anything that resembled disappointment. She simply listened, holding his hands like the faithful companion she'd been for nearly forty years. Into Kevin's pause, she nodded. "I have thought on the contradiction too. That in spite of the dark life he couldn't find his way out of, your dad left behind a blessing. One that changed our lives."

"I want to say it out loud. I need to—even though I don't know where he is now and am frankly scared to imagine." Kevin turned his attention back to the trees. "I'm grateful, Dad. Thank you for providing me and my family with a life that could have looked very different otherwise."

Seemed like practicing gratitude shouldn't take forty years to get around to. But it had. Seemed like it shouldn't take such an emotional toll. But it did.

Even so, as exhaustion crept in and his intuitive wife looped her arm through his and guided him back home, Kevin was glad to finally lay that burden to rest. It certainly had been a long time coming.

Helen peeked into the master bedroom a half hour after they'd returned from their walk. Kevin had finished his cider and was now dozing peacefully. For several minutes she watched the rise and fall of his chest, each puff of air eliciting gratitude from her heart.

Life was a beautiful gift.

She bent to press a soft kiss to his temple, then picked up the empty mug and slipped away. Once in the kitchen, she made herself a fresh mug of steaming spiced orange tea and then settled at the table. In front of her waited the large picture book she'd dug free from a lower cabinet. With a cautious finger, she traced the edge of the front cover and then gingerly opened to the beginning.

The date on the front flap read 1989. Helen turned the page and was catapulted into decades past.

Jackson had turned two and had undergone his second surgery. The stitches beneath his nose and down his lip looked like tiny spiders trailing his sweet little face. Even so, most of the photographs that captured him revealed eyes that held mischief.

Though he looked like his father, Jackson would grow up to act like his mother.

Oh, how Helen loved a good belly laugh! And she was certainly the ornery sort. One only needed to ask her older neighbor from her growing-up years. Tilly Knolls used to call Helen Chase their very own little Dennis the Menace. From pouring milk on the floor in Ms. Knolls's kitchen so that she could share a snack with the woman's kitties, to sneaking out to fork the neighborhood lawns as a teenager, Helen *loved* fun.

Kevin had said it was one of the things that attracted him to her the most. His dark life had desperately needed fun.

Jackson was Helen's mini-me—and it was a good thing, because he needed humor in the unique struggles he'd encounter in life. Sometimes, though, Helen had forgotten that her son had come with an abundance of laughing fortitude. Sometimes that mama bear in her had been a little much—even to the detriment of her other sons on occasion.

But in those pictures, she saw only a two-year-old making faces at the camera, somehow managing to do so around those stitches.

In those pictures she also saw three older boys making messes, and grinning like little monkeys, and living the boy life like natural-born pros, oblivious to the tininess of their home or the oddity that all four shared one bedroom. And in those pictures she saw the backdrop of that cabin. The one Kevin had forced himself to adopt as home once again and then fix up the best he could on the very limited amount of money that they'd had.

Somewhere midway through the photo album, she came to two moments in time that were encased in her memory with perfect clarity. First was Kevin's birthday—she couldn't remember which birthday, but she remembered so many other details. Namely, the fact that on that day, as she had decorated the homemade cake she'd cooled on the counter, she experienced a sudden bout of nausea.

After barely making it to the toilet to empty her stomach, realization dawned. The recent tiredness. The strange dreams. And only the day before, a sudden tingle in her breasts.

She was pregnant for the fifth time.

Though she'd felt guilty over it even at the first tear, Helen had cried. Seven years, five babies, and, thanks to massive hospital bills, she and Kevin were as poor as they'd been when they'd gotten married.

As Helen studied the pictures glued to the album's paper, she fixed on the one that her mother or Elizabeth must have taken—the one of just her and Kevin. He looked happy, her in his lap and his arms wrapped around her. At that point he'd been oblivious to their next stork visit. But Helen . . . Helen looked pensive.

It'd been a near breaking point for her. She'd loved her boys, but she couldn't imagine mothering *five* children. They were okay in that little cabin that Kevin had fixed up, but how could they fit *five* children in one room.

What if this one was a girl?

What if this one, like Jackson, was born with special (expensive) medical needs?

What if she broke?

What if Kevin broke?

In that faded photo, Helen could read all of those fears as if they were printed in bold captions below.

As she sat at the large wooden table Kevin had built for her, the steaming tea cooling in one hand and her other hand fingering those memories, Helen paused, shut her eyes, and turned her heart toward gratitude. Because on this side of the album, Helen of the present knew what frightened and tired Helen of the past didn't.

She knew the rest of the story.

CHAPTER TWELVE

(in which God provides)

T he boys ran around the front yard, piling sticks they'd gathered from the trees, determined to make a fort. Matthew directed as usual, and Jacob countered, as usual. The younger two carried out orders from both. Three cute little dark-haired mischief makers and one blondie, ages seven to two.

Ah, but she did adore them, even if she spent her days mostly trying to keep them alive while not losing her sanity.

From the window over the kitchen sink, Helen stopped peeling potatoes and watched her boys at work. As she did, she lowered the peeler and covered the small bulge of her womb.

She needed to tell Kevin. At this rate she'd be showing soon and he'd figure it out on his own. Likely, he'd be hurt that she'd kept it from him. If she could just find the measure of peace about another baby, maybe she'd be able to let the small inklings of joy tucked in her heart grow, and then she'd be able to tell him without crying.

What was wrong with her anyway? Children were a blessing.

But this cabin was so small—and their budget was smaller still. How would they make this work?

The phone rang, jarring Helen out of her melancholy. She set the wet, half-peeled potato in the sink, wiped her hands on a dish towel, and moved to answer it.

"How's the love of my life?" Though he often would call before leaving the mill to ask her if she needed anything from town, Helen wondered what was going on. Kevin sounded particularly happy that early Friday evening.

"I'm good. Getting supper going."

"Well, stop." His voice was firm command. "The boys are going to the Claytons' tonight. Uncle Dave is making his homemade pizza."

"Oh." Huh. That was odd. Not that the Claytons would invite them over—that happened often—but that it was so last minute. "But the potatoes are almost all peeled."

"Bag them. Or whatever." Now Kevin sounded all eager boy. "My lovely wife needs a break, and I'm whisking her away for the night."

"What?"

"Pack something for the coast."

"Kevin. We can't afford that."

"Woman, don't argue."

"Kevin."

"I mean it, Helen. You've been off lately. You need a break, and I've already made the arrangements. It's only for one night."

Such a kind and thoughtful gesture from her husband, who over the past several years had grown into a tremendously kind and thoughtful man. Kevin was a hard worker, a good provider, and more and more a godly leader of their home. Though when she'd married him, she done so with tremendous fear, because that version of Kevin had been unstable and captive to a budding addiction, now Helen was ever thankful for the man she called her own.

The last thing she wanted was to disappoint his obviously eager plans. But an urge to cry and to simply spit out what had been weighing on her was nearly overwhelming.

"I'll be home in fifteen minutes. Can you have the boys' stuff packed? I'll take them straight over to the Claytons."

"Kevin, I really don't think—"

"Helen, please don't spoil this."

How could she let him down when he sounded like that? So sweetly determined, with that undertone of longing. Helen had no idea how he intended to pay for a night out—food, hotel, gas? They had zero free-spending money. And with baby number five on the way . . .

Kevin didn't know about that yet.

Perhaps after he had the boys settled with George and Elizabeth, she would be able to talk Kevin into a stay-over at home. It'd be sort of the same—just the two of them.

Yes. That would work. "Okay, hon. I'll get the boys ready."

"And pack for yourself."

She couldn't promise him that. "I'll see you soon."

Just over a half hour later, they stood in the middle of their tiny kitchen, sans four small children, face to face and neither one budging.

"The reservations aren't refundable, Helen."

Helen rubbed her back. "This is so unlike you. You know our budget."

"I know things that you don't." He winked at her. "But I'm sure excited to tell you."

Perhaps he'd gotten a raise at work—and that was something to be celebrated! But not a couple hundred dollars' worth of celebration. Not when bigger bills were looming on the horizon.

Sighing, her hands fell limp at her side. Time to just be out with it. "Kevin, I'm pregnant." Her throat swelled as she got the news into the open, and a giant tear leaked from one eye.

Lips parted, brown eyes wide, her husband stared at her for more breaths than she could count.

Oh dear.

"But . . . but we . . . we were preventing that. Right?"

Helen bit her lip and looked to the floor. "It didn't work, I guess." Shouldn't be that shocking. Birth control had failed them before.

The space between them filled with more awkward silence with each passing breath.

Then his low, quiet chuckle startled her out of her misery, and her attention zipped right back to his face. Kevin crossed the four feet of space between them and cupped her face with both hands. "Is that what's been going on with you?"

Blinking, a handful of tears escaped. "I didn't know how to tell you."

"I thought maybe you'd grown tired of me." He winked and then brushed her lips with his. "Now I know. I'm relieved." He wrapped a firm embrace around her and cradled her against his chest.

Helen settled in, savoring the warmth of him, the strong rhythm of his heartbeat, and the comforting scent of wood shavings and the Avon aftershave she'd given him for his birthday.

"Should I tell you my secret now?" he whispered.

Helen sniffed. "Is it a good one?"

"Not as good as yours. But yes."

Her heart puddled at his words. All this time she'd been worried that he wouldn't be happy. Perhaps because rather than wonder at the miracle of another baby, she had worried instead. She hadn't been able to imagine that Kevin wouldn't do the same, and she'd felt certain that he would feel even more pressure.

She lay a palm against the steady beat of his heart. "Then tell me."

Kevin leaned back and looked down at her. "Only if you promise to be an obedient wife after and come with me on this getaway."

Helen sighed. "I just don't—"

With pinched fingers, Kevin gently stilled her lips. "A nod will do."

Seemed she had no choice, so she complied.

Kevin replaced his fingers against her lips with another kiss and then grinned. "I wanted to tell you at dinner tonight. But this will work, I suppose." His smile widened, and he reached into his back pocket. Between two fingers, he held a legal sized envelope, which he placed into her hands. "Read it."

A promotion, certainly. Helen summoned enthusiasm because truly, it would be good news. Not reckless-spending-level good news, but good news nonetheless.

It took less than a sentence for her to discover that she'd been grossly mistaken.

This was not a promotion at all. This was . . . astounding.

After swiftly taking in the rest of the document, Helen looked up at her husband, stunned. "Will you agree?"

"If you say yes."

Blinking, she looked back down at the paper, half expecting to discover that'd she'd misread it. Surely she wasn't understanding it correctly . . . "We would keep half the property?"

"That's the deal. And I would be foreman on the builds. The job comes with a significant pay raise. And the added benefit of experience, so that when it comes to our house—"

Her eyes grew wider. "Our house?"

Pure delight made his smile glow. "Yes. We would build new as well."

Helen's head swam. This couldn't be real, could it? She looked back at the sum at the bottom—an offer for the ten acres of land across the creek, on the other side of the dirt road. "Why would he pay so much money for ten worthless acres?"

Their land wasn't farmable. There weren't trace mineral deposits to mine. That section didn't even have the benefit of the running creek. It was mountainous, uneven land nobody wanted.

Except Mr. Glasco, the owner of the mill where Kevin worked, apparently wanted it.

"The county has allowed residential plotting on that side of the road." Kevin reached for the papers Helen held in her hands and brought the back one she hadn't yet looked at to the front. "They've reduced the requirements to build a house from ten acres to one in that zoning. So Mr. Glasco can subdivide that section ten times, build ten nice homes, and make a tidy profit. If we're willing to sell to him." He set aside the letter and loosely gripped Helen's arms. "Mr. Glasco wants it to be a good deal for both of us, and I think it is. We don't have the capital or the experience to subdivide and build, but he does. He doesn't have the land, but we do. And the offer is more than fair. I checked, Helen. It's a very good offer."

"Who would buy those ten houses?"

The gleam in Kevin's eyes only danced more, despite her clear doubt. "Glasco sees the tourist industry taking off in the near future. With the marina going in at Sugar Creek reservoir, he says it's only a matter of time . . ."

Could that be right? Helen didn't know, but either way, the bigger question was, could this be real?

The shock hadn't worn off. Helen stood there gaping at her husband. "We would keep this side and build a new house?"

"A bigger house. Big enough for *five* children." Kevin winked again and moved to slip his hands at her waist. "Five beautiful Murphy children, which clearly we are very good at making."

A giddy, uncontrollable giggle bubbled in her belly and wiggled out of her chest. "Kevin!"

He joined in her laughter and swept her into his arms. "Helen." Then he twirled her around that tiny kitchen.

"I was moping! Telling God we couldn't afford more babies, and what was He thinking? And all this time, He had things worked out." Breathless from dancing and laughing and crying, Helen sagged against him.

Holding her steady, Kevin rubbed her back. "All this time, He's had us covered." Then he curled around her and kissed her neck. "So will you come away with me, my dove? My bride?"

"Yes," she whispered.

Helen turned to the last page in that aged album. In the middle, as the solitary photo, was an enlarged copy of the capstone of that year. The Murphy seven stood in front of the deck of a beautifully crafted, big new home. Kevin and Helen in the middle, his arms around her, and her arms holding a blanketed baby boy they'd named Tyler. Both were grinning wildly. Flanking them were four growing boys. Three with dark hair favoring their dad. One blond, who looked like her.

Sitting there, in that very house thirty-some years later, Helen still felt the wonder of it wash over her.

God had provided an unbelievable abundance. And he'd done it, as unlikely as it had seemed, through Kevin's dad.

Closing the album, Helen let her eyes fall shut. "Thank you," she whispered. To God. And to Tom Murphy.

CHAPTER THIRTEEN

(in which Kevin is mush)

"Hey, Dad." Matt walked into the basement family room, a mug in each hand. "What are you working on here?"

Comfortable in the plush recliner, a card table pushed up against it, Kevin looked up to his oldest son. Was there a touch of gray at Matt's temple? How could that be?

Kevin brushed aside the sense that he was much older than he'd been a month ago, before the heart attack. Matt had been thirty-nine years old before Kevin had bypass surgery, and he was thirty-nine years old now. Time had not slipped that much.

"Hi Matt. I'm trying to work this puzzle."

Matt chuckled knowingly. "Not really your speed, is it?" He would know—puzzles weren't exactly Matt's cup of joe either. They preferred power tools, big impact, and projects that stayed done—not broken down and replaced into a box.

"Your mom says I'll be good at it. And that it's about time I learn to sit still for more than two minutes at a time."

Laughing again, Matt pulled a chair up to the opposite side of the table. "She's one to talk."

Meeting his son's amused gaze, Kevin chuckled along with him. Exactly. Helen was a honeybee sort—always flitting around doing the next thing, happily buzzing along as she went. "What are you up to?"

Motioning toward the mug he'd placed in front of Kevin, Matt then sat back. "I've been banished to the basement as well."

"Banished?"

"Seems I am useless with the trees once they are out of the ground. Something about no eye for color schemes and being too much in a rush." He shrugged, as if he had no idea what that meant. "So Lauren and Kenzie and Mom kicked me out of the greenhouse while they work on decorating them, and sent me with the consolation of hot cider to see that you're resting."

"I'm tired of all the resting."

"I can imagine." Matt lifted his mug to his mouth.

"What are the little girls up to?"

"Jacob and Jackson offered to take all the kids to the Storm for dipped cones before Jackson and Kenz head back down the mountain. As soon as Mom and Lauren wrap things up, we'll pack up and head over the pass toward home as well."

Kevin shook his head in wonder. "Jacob and Jackson. Who would have thought?"

"Divine intervention." Amusement lit Matt's eyes.

Kevin palmed the warm mug Matt had delivered and sipped the steaming liquid. Undertones of orange, cranberry, and cinnamon mingled with the apple of Helen's homemade cider. He paused for a moment to savor the drink.

Man, his wife could do amazing things in the kitchen. He could live without her tea though—and he was ever so glad to have had that out there now.

For several comfortable moments, quiet settled between the pair. Both put their attention to the puzzle, searching out matches from the one thousand pieces scattered over the table.

Seemed a crazy thing to do to Kevin, cutting a perfectly good image into a bunch of weird-shaped pieces, mixing them all up, only to spend hours putting it back together again.

But there he was, puzzling. And reflecting on divine intervention.

Kevin stopped searching for matches and looked at his oldest son. He'd been three when Kevin had wrecked his truck—perhaps old enough to remember it, and everything else. Had Kevin ever asked him?

He hadn't. Perhaps fear had held him back. Or simply the desire to move forward and embrace the new life he'd been given. But that day he wanted to know.

"Do you remember me being in the hospital when you were little?"

Matt's attention lifted from the table, and he blinked as a searching expression pressed on his brows. "I knew you were, I think." He shrugged. "It's blurry at best. I remember Uncle Dave staying with Jacob and me quite a bit for a time, but maybe that was when Connor was born."

"Those events happened the same year."

"Oh." Matt held a questioning look and waited.

"You knew I wrecked my truck though, right?"

"There's a vague memory of that, yes. Though I think maybe it's more from you telling me about it later—when I was a teenager or something. You said you'd been drinking and rolled your truck. I remember that. You told all of us boys, as a warning."

Kevin nodded, his study back on the puzzle. He had done that much at least, because he wanted his sons to know that drunk driving was a really, really bad idea. That wasn't what he wanted to know right then though.

He cleared his throat and made himself look at Matt again. "Do you remember me before?" A slow burn crept into his face. "Do you remember me as a drunk?"

Gentle compassion filled Matt's dark eyes, and he shook his head. "I remember the man sitting in a chair every morning, Bible open on one knee. I remember being in footy pajamas—the same kind my girls wear now—and being lifted onto your lap. I remember sitting there listening to you read to me and hoping I'd grow up to be like you."

A thick lump swelled in Kevin's throat. He swallowed against it as heat stung his eyes. "I wasn't always that man. There was a time I desperately hoped you would *never* become like me."

"But you became that man, Dad." Matt reached across the table and gripped Kevin's elbow. "You are that man now. You're still the man that all of us look up to. All of us try to be like you."

"By divine intervention." Kevin could barely muster the words out. "By God's grace."

Matt nodded and squeezed his arm again. Sometimes there weren't words. Or maybe they just weren't necessary.

As silence settled between them again and they fixed their attention back to the puzzle, Kevin regained his emotions while at the same time lifting the wonder of his redeemed life back up to his Savior.

Great are You, Lord, and greatly to be praised! Your greatness is unsearchable. Help me never to forget . . .

He saw a match and moved to secure the piece into place.

"Has Connor talked to you?" Matt kept his focus on the pieces as he asked.

An interesting jump in topics. Kevin eyed his oldest for a moment. Perhaps it wasn't much of a stretch in topics at all. "We talk. Was there something specific you were thinking he needed to say to me?"

"He's going to propose." Matt met Kevin's stare.

Kevin blinked. No, Connor hadn't said as much. It hurt that he hadn't.

"He'd like to at Christmas, when they're here."

"No, he didn't say." Kevin breathed through the squeeze of pain that fact provoked. It was his own fault, and he knew it. He hadn't exactly been supportive or excited when Connor had talked to him about his interest in his new neighbor. Instead, Kevin had urged an abundance of caution—probably with too much force.

Grief can make you do things that maybe aren't for the best, son. And this woman has her own baggage to deal with. Just . . . go slow.

Maybe it had been valid advice, but Kevin knew for certain that he'd spoken from a place of distrust. In God, mostly, regarding Connor. But maybe even in Connor. The wiser path likely would have been to go and meet Jade Beck and her children before offering a commentary on any of it.

But Kevin hadn't done that, and Connor clearly felt that Kevin disapproved.

He'd not been that man Matt had just praised—the one his sons followed after. He'd been locked up in his own disappointment, captive to a faithlessness that had wounded his son.

Sadly, they'd been through this before, when Connor had married Sadie. Helen had been so discomfited about it. She hated the idea that Connor would marry a woman out of a sense of duty and miss the wild bliss of marital love.

They had underestimated God's loving plan for hurting, ordinary people, and it had caused a rift in their relationship with Connor for a time. Blessedly, all that had smoothed out, and Helen and Kevin had both come to adore Sadie. So much so that letting her go had been excruciating.

Now, here they were again. Underestimating Connor's good judgment and, very likely, God's extraordinary ability to architect something breathtaking from reclaimed lives.

Matt braced his forearms against the table. "Dad, Jade is a really nice woman."

Tyler had said the same thing right before Kevin got a ride in an ambulance. He was apparently not being the man his sons expected him to be on this. And they were right.

Surrender, son. That's what this battle is. George's voice echoed softly in the place of safekeeping of precious memories. Wise men listen to wise men, so Kevin gripped the long-past instruction firmly.

Kevin nodded. "Ty also said that. I'll call Connor and bring it up."

"It won't upset you if he proposes?"

"Connor's a grown man with a good heart. I'm sure he's prayed about this."

"He has. I really think they both have. And truly, Dad. They're good together—Connor and Jade and the kids. Your approval would mean a lot to Connor."

Kevin took another drink and then nodded. "I won't be upset. I'll be happy for them."

"Even though it's your anniversary?"

At that, Kevin grinned an impish smile. "If it's Christmas day, it'll be my second honeymoon. So frankly, I won't much care."

Matt laughed. "I don't need any details, Dad." Rubbing his neck, which was amusingly tinged red, Matt glanced toward the window that gave a small view of the backyard.

Watching Matt squirm with discomfort, the way the boys did as young teens when Kevin would take Helen in close and make a show of kissing her noisily, provoked Kevin's laugh. "Come on now, son. You're a grown man with a wife of your own."

Eyeing him with a smirk, Matt shook his head. "I don't buy it anyway. You'll be just over three weeks out from bypass surgery and have a houseful of Murphys for Christmas morning. You're all talk. I was thinking about that though." He shot a cautionary look at Kevin. "Your anniversary, not the honeymoon part. Let's just leave that one between you and Mom so I don't feel weird."

"Thanks for clarifying."

"What if Ty and I put up a wooden arbor near the mouth of the ridge trail? Lauren and Kenzie could make it special with evergreens and such. Mom so loves the outdoors."

Kevin thought on that. "She does, but she doesn't love to be cold." It was December, after all, and they'd planned for the evening. "I think the sunroom is still the best choice. In front of the fireplace."

Matt nodded an easy concession. "We'll have our wives concoct a reason for her to clear out of here that morning then. Which, by the way, will be no small feat—especially since they can't all be in on it. Lauren and Kenz will have to stay here to make sure everything looks good. Budging Mom out of the kitchen on a holiday will take a herculean effort."

There was truth to that. "I could always fake another heart attack."

"Don't you dare." Matt pinned him with a glare. "No one would be impressed by that sort of stunt."

Nodding, Kevin went back to searching for matching pieces. Maybe there was something to this puzzling thing. It was a distraction from boredom. And a pathway into reflection. Not bad things at all.

"Connor says Jade loves the bench and arbor at the lookout over the lake." Matt dipped into a fresh topic. "Said that little Miss Lily has decided someday she'll get married there."

A small grin poked on Kevin's mouth as he thought on that small project. "Do you remember putting it up with me?"

Matt matched his happy, nostalgic look. "I do. My first project on the road with you."

The first of many projects Kevin had done with his older boys—several of them for Harold Appleton at the Lake Shore Lodge. Kevin had loved that he could take his sons to jobs. That he could teach them carpentry skills, the unique dignity of work, and the love of God's great outdoors, all at the same time. He'd loved working alongside his sons.

Some days he really, really missed that. Grown men now, they had families of their own. Jobs that kept them away. Lives that had branched out
from beyond Kevin's everyday view.

There had been a time when Kevin had sincerely hoped and planned
that his boys would continue to work with him. Murphy and Sons. Then,
when Kevin was out of it, Murphy Brothers. That hadn't happened, and it
wasn't going to.

Help me let it go . . .

Kevin was proud of the men his sons had become, and he was grateful
they could pursue their lives in a way that brought them joy. He put his
mind toward that rather than the niggling disappointment of dreams come
and gone.

After all, he *had* given them a legacy. Matt had just said so—and it
was a much richer, so much more important inheritance than any family
business ever could have been.

The sound of footfalls against the stairs brought Kevin out of his head,
and he turned to find Kate, Jacob's wife, rounding the base of the steps,
then striding toward him. When he connected with her blue eyes, she
grinned.

"Daddy Murph." Kate leaned over the back of the chair and wrapped a
quick hug around his shoulders.

His heart lightened. There was no measure to the tender joy it brought
Kevin to have Kate call him *Daddy Murph*. For all the strain that had been
in his and Helen's relationship with Jacob and Kate the first few years of
their marriage, there was this beautiful, rare closeness between them now.

It was a unique bond—his and Kate's. Once Kate had braved honesty
with them about her past—her roots—Kevin had opened his own history
to both Jacob and Kate with a depth that he really hadn't shared with the
other boys. His story and Kate's story were so similar, and he understood

with a distinctive intimacy why she'd worked the deception the way she'd done

Jacob had asked Kevin once, after hearing the whole of Kevin's young life, why he hadn't told them all his story when they were young. Was he trying to shield them from the past? Was he still ashamed of it?

Some things are just hard, Jacob. Hard to live through. Hard to remember. Hard to talk about. There was so much humiliation in that life. To be honest, I just really don't like to go back to it.

Kate had nodded with full understanding. Not long after that, she'd taken to calling Kevin *Daddy Murph*—a name Lauren had tagged him with a few years before. It meant more than Kevin or Helen could put into words to have Kate soften to them, adopt them as her own.

Especially Kevin—because Kate didn't have a dad. He'd known how deeply that affected a soul and was honored to become hers. It was a position he would never take for granted.

"You're resting like you're supposed to, right?" Kate propped her hands on her hips and put on her mom face.

A question on loop. "Here I sit. Did Helen send you?"

Kate grinned. "No. I snuck into the house, and Mama Helen didn't catch me. Did you find the box?"

"What's this?" Matt looked up at Kate.

Kate's eyebrows bounced. "The hat box."

"Ah." Matt nodded with a conspirator's wink. "*The* hat."

"I found it." Kevin moved to push himself out of the recliner.

"Oh no." Kate pushed on his shoulder until he sat back down. "Use your words."

"You've been mothering littles too much. *Use your words.*" Kevin rolled his eyes and shook his head as he mocked her.

Matt chuckled. "Kate, I love that you have proven to be Dad's match. Don't let up." Then he looked at Kevin. "And, Dad, just tell us where the box is, and we'll take it from there."

With a good-natured growl, Kevin eyed them both. "Fine. Officer Bossy and Officer Funhater."

Kate burst out laughing.

"Shush. You want to be found out?"

She covered her mouth and let her eyes do the laughing.

"Now." Kevin pointed the direction from which Kate had come. "In the storage room under the stairs, behind the safe, you'll find a baby-blue box."

"That's it?" Kate said.

"That's it." Kevin nodded. "You girls will see to the rest, right?"

"Operation Christmas Eve Bride is in full swing." Kate kissed her fingertips and then tapped Kevin's forehead with them. "Trust your girls, Daddy Murph. We've got this. And it's going to be the best thing ever."

And then she whisked herself out.

Matt followed Kate's trail with his eyes and waited until the door to the storage room creaked open. Then he looked back at Kevin. "It's a good thing you weren't allowed to have daughters until they were grown-ups."

"What?" He and Helen had actually tried for a daughter . . . "Why?"

"You're mush, Pops. Total and complete mush."

"Nah." Kevin waved off his son's accusation.

But though he wouldn't admit it out loud, Matt wasn't wrong, and Kevin well knew it. He flat out adored his daughters-in-law, and those sweet little granddaughters pretty much had him trained.

Papa, we get ice cream?

It's nine in the morning, Bobbie Joy. Probably better not.

But ice cream is 'licious!"

That's true. Let's go.

Bobbie Joy had been two or three years old at that time. Even then she'd owned him. Just one of many proofs. When it came to the girls who had planted in his heart, he was a hopeless spoiler.

And he loved it.

CHAPTER FOURTEEN

(in which plans are discussed)

"Dad." Connor's surprise carried in his voice as he answered the phone. "How are you?"

"Good. And before you ask, I'm resting like I'm supposed to."

"That was just on the tip of my tongue." Connor chuckled. "How did you know?"

"It's standard issue apparently."

"We'd like you to hang around awhile longer."

"I think that's the plan. But we'll do as God wills." Kevin lowered into his leather chair and looked out the large window to his left. A nearly full moon lit the cold, clear night.

"Everything okay?" Connor asked.

"Yeah."

"Plans are in full motion?"

"They are. The girls have taken over, so I think we're in good hands."

"And Brandon . . . are the legal papers going to come through in time?"

"He says it's done. Good to go." Pride infused Kevin's voice. This direction was not one he'd foreseen for his introverted son. But the more he thought on it, the more it made sense. Brandon never needed attention—he didn't like it. He didn't need other people's approval, and he wasn't driven to make a name for himself. Megan was more than enough companionship for him, and he was satisfied with a job well done. Praise for it was entirely unnecessary.

It seemed like a backward confirmation—that what Brandon would do going forward wasn't for his own ego. If he was to preach, it would be by the Spirit's strength, and it would be done for the glory of God.

After lingering in the pool of joy that reflection provided, Kevin shifted his thoughts back to the purpose at hand. "I called to talk about you though."

"Me?" Connor paused. "Whatever you need from me, Dad, just name it."

"I need you to tell me how you really feel."

"Uh . . ." He could picture Connor rubbing the back of his neck—it'd been his nervous tell since Connor had been six. "Feel about what?"

"You know what. Start talking, and I promise this time I'm listening. *Really* listening."

"Is . . . is this about Jade?"

"Yes. And you."

"What did Matt say?"

"Never mind what Matt said—except that he implied I've disappointed you. I'm sorry for that."

Connor swallowed audibly—a sound that nicked Kevin's heart because it meant that, yes, Kevin had injured Connor with his cool reserve about this new romance. He should have rejoiced that God had brought healing and new love into his son's life. Having been told that she loved Jesus and wanted this fresh start to look more like what God would have it be, Kevin should have been ready to meet and welcome this woman, rather than hold her and Connor at arm's length.

"I failed you, Connor, and I'm sorry," Kevin mustered through a hoarse whisper.

"She's . . . she's really wonderful, Dad. I promise you and mom will like her."

"I believe you."

"She's nothing like Sadie." Timid warning snaked in his voice.

"Does that bother you?"

"No. I prefer it, I think. It bothered her at first, when she realized it."

"But not now?"

"I love her as she is, and we're happy."

"And the kids? Are they good with everything?"

Connor chuckled. "For a while she and I backed everything up because we weren't sure how the kids would take it. Specifically, how Kellen would respond. But then they did the craziest thing." He stopped to laugh again.

The sound of Connor's joy sparked something that felt like a brand-new sprout of life in Kevin's heart. Suddenly, he couldn't wait to meet Jade and her children. He couldn't wait to welcome these people who had filled his son's heart. "What crazy thing was that?"

"They parent-trapped us."

It took a minute for Kevin to understand, but then a few scenes from an old flick that Helen had liked blipped in his mind. He chuckled. "They set you up?"

"Oh, they worked pretty hard at it and were proud as lions when it seemed their not-so-sneaky efforts paid off."

Kevin tried to imagine Reid being sneaky, trying to set up his dad with a woman. He couldn't muster it. "I can't wait to hear all about it from the kids."

"Lily will give you every detail you ever wanted and a few you didn't know you needed."

"She's a chatty one, hmm?"

"Well, if she likes you. But she'll be polite either way. She's quite a kid."

"And Kellen?"

"Kellen is a tough one to crack. But I think we're on good footing now. His dad has left him with a lot of damage—a lot of anger. So if he's aloof, just be patient."

Kevin understood all too well how that went. In the pause that landed between them, he prayed for the boy's wounded heart and asked for wisdom. For himself and for Connor, who would more likely than not, and sooner rather than later, become stepdad to both kids.

"Dad, I'm going to marry Jade." Connor's proclamation was so . . . so Connor. Resolute. Not a question, not a distant hope. A firm decision made from careful consideration and intentional prayer. Nothing—not even Kevin's disapproval—would sway him.

Good thing Kevin didn't disapprove. "Have you asked her?"

"I have plans."

"For Christmas?"

"Yes."

"What can we do to help?"

"Welcome her. Like you did with all the girls. She's terribly nervous about coming. Has even offered to drive up by herself the day after Christmas so things aren't awkward."

"Would she rather spend Christmas with her family?"

"They've done Christmas on New Year's Eve for years, so we're planning on that together. She's just scared you won't like her—that you'll disapprove because she's divorced, or you won't like her kids, or five hundred other bad possibilities that keep her up at night." Connor paused to take a breath. "Please, Dad. Take her in. Hear her story, not just that she's divorced. Know her heart, because it's really beautiful. If you would just—"

"Connor." Kevin waited for Connor to come to a full stop. "No more worrying. Not for you, not for Jade. You're a good man with a heart for God. I trust you. I trust your judgment. I'm sorry it seemed that I didn't before. It wasn't about you at all, really. It was me wrestling with God. If you love Jade and you want to marry her, and you have God's peace about it, then you have my blessing. And I promise I'll love her and her kids. It shouldn't be hard—Matt says I'm mush."

The laugh that Connor puffed over the digital air sounded like a mix of humor and deep relief. "You are putty in the girls' hands, there's no denying that."

"Then tell Jade she has nothing to worry about. We can't wait to spend Christmas with her."

"And you won't mind if I propose?"

"You asked her father, right?"

Connor's tone turned to mocked offense. "Who do you think you're dealing with here?"

"Then propose on Christmas. Your mother's romantic heart will melt."

It was the truth. And Kevin couldn't wait to see it.

CHAPTER FIFTEEN

(in which there is a full house)

"**M**att said it was a good thing we didn't have girls."

Lying on her back beneath the pile of warm covers, her fingers woven with Kevin's, Helen turned her head and peered through the dim night between them. She couldn't make out his expression, and his voice was neutral. But he wouldn't have brought it up if something about Matt's comment hadn't stuck in his heart somewhere.

Helen turned and levered up on one arm. "Why did he say that?"

"Because I'm putty with the girls." He chuckled as he released her hand and moved to wrap an arm around her

Helen snuggled against him. "That's the truth. You're such a softy."

The low rumble that came from his chest was one of contentment. For several breaths he simply held her in the darkness. Then he kissed her forehead. "Does it ever disappoint you?"

Helen chuckled, loving that his tenderness still made the tiny hairs at the back of her neck prickle. "No. But it was sure fun trying."

Beneath her palm, his heart kicked, making her sure that his recollection of those days had been kept secure in his treasury of cherished memories. She allowed herself to indulge in those sweet and intimate moments between them.

Tyler's third birthday had been a success.

Helen had baked a chocolate cake and decorated it with a frosting Big Bird in the middle. Tyler had loved it, as well as his present, Big Bird Story Magic. Helen had selected that gift almost selfishly. That talking bird would keep her younger boys entranced with a story for at least thirty minutes, and she could get something done before the older boys came home from school.

Life had evened out over the past decade. Helen felt like they'd hit their stride and were doing well. She and Kevin had celebrated twelve years of marriage, and they'd found a groove parenting these five boys. It all felt . . . ordained.

But for one thing.

That night, after all the boys had been jammied, storied, prayed with, and tucked into bed, she'd slipped into a nightie she'd known Kevin would appreciate.

"Hello, what's this?" His low tone, pleased and welcoming, greeted her as she slid onto her knees beside him between the sheets. "It's not *my* birthday."

She met his mouth with a kiss that promised more and then pushed him back. "I want to ask you something."

"Ah, so we're using our assets, are we?" He winked. "Obviously I'll say yes now."

Helen smirked, feeling sexy and wanted and more daring than usual under that warm gaze. But first things first.

"You have to honestly think on this one, Kevin."

"It's a little late for you to throw that in." His fingers grazed the exposed skin of her shoulder as he traced her form down to her hip and then sat up to kiss the line he'd just traced on her arm. "Like a man could have rational thoughts with this at his fingertips."

"I want another baby."

That snapped him out of it. Kevin dropped back to his two stacked pillows and stared at her, wide eyed. "Come again?"

"I want to try for a girl."

He blinked.

"Just one more and that's all, babe. After all, we've figured out five. How hard could one more be? Besides, then it'll be an even number, so we won't end up with a weird middle child."

After blinking three more times, his slow, sultry smile made its way back onto his mouth. "You're seducing me to make another baby?"

Biting her lip and blushing furiously, Helen nodded.

"You think we can handle one more?"

Again, she nodded.

In one sweeping motion, he had her in his arms and on her back, his lips a soft tease against hers. "You certainly know how to get what you want, Mrs. Murphy."

With a palm against his wildly beating heart, she pushed against him. "But do *you* want another one?"

That delicious low chuckle rumbled from his throat. "Yeah. A daughter might be fun." He moved to nuzzle her neck, stopping to whisper in her ear. "So we start tonight, right?"

She didn't have to answer.

"That night is still one of my favorite memories, Helen," Kevin murmured into her hair.

She still blushed at her brazen tactic, though clearly Kevin hadn't minded one bit.

"I was afraid you would be disappointed when I saw that Brandon was not going to be a Brooklyn before the nurse announced he was a boy."

Smiling with contentment, Helen shook her head against Kevin's shoulder. "It was love at first sight."

"You said that with all of them."

"It was true with all of them."

Kevin stroked the forearm she'd draped over him. "We still ended up with an odd number—and a weird middle child."

"Jackson was born unique. And he's fine with it. Anyway, he's a perfectly hilarious sort of weird."

"Hmm . . . that's true." After an interlude of silence, Kevin chuckled softly. "Remember how you told me about Brayden?"

Again, Helen smiled. "That was my favorite tell."

They had agreed six was it for them. Their house was full, their family complete.

Famous last words.

When Helen realized number seven was on the way, she'd almost shrugged it off. Of their seven boys, only two had been planned babies—a thing that was noted by her mother with a wry comment—*You do know how this works, right dear?*—so by then, she was used to that sort of surprise. However, unlike the other unexpected pregnancies, this one wouldn't throw them into financial crisis.

By God's grace, the Murphys had landed on their feet, and they were doing okay.

But she had been a little anxious about telling Kevin. So she'd reverted to humor to share the news. On an evening when the boys had gone to spend the night at George and Elizabeth Clayton's, Helen had made one of Kevin's favorite dishes—lasagna—and also prepped a paper sack. After he enjoyed their intimate meal for two, she pulled it up from beneath the table and handed it to him.

"What's this?" He asked.

"Open it."

He eyed her with a suspicious gleam. "Your surprises are usually a long-term investment."

Something like that. Helen gestured to her offering, then sat back and watched while he unfolded the top of the brown bag.

Then he tugged out the notecard she'd penned with a Sharpie. "I'm told you're the best one around, so I can't wait to meet you, D—" Kevin's eyes cut from the note card to Helen, and for a breath they held on her. Disbelieving and a little wild. "Daddy?"

Helen stretched out a smile—her silent *surprise!*

"Another baby?"

"We're really good at making them." Her anxiety notched up at his stunned reaction.

And then . . . then Kevin laughed. He laughed and laughed until there were tears leaking from his eyes, and Helen laughed with him.

"Seven?" he said between gasps.

"Seven."

"What if this one is another boy?"

"Then we will need seven brides for seven brothers someday."

Which had been exactly the case. And it had been glorious.

Kevin turned onto his side and cradled Helen in his arms. "I regret nothing, my darling wife."

"Me neither." She stretched to kiss his lips. The same lips she'd been kissing for the last forty years—which was not long enough.

Kevin resolved to enjoy these slower days. Because *for everything there is a season.* This was his time to keep. A season to savor the memories and these quiet, still moments where his body would recover. So much of him had revolted against that idea.

But God ordained seasons and times. It was for Kevin to surrender, to embrace, and to praise.

And as he trained himself to do those things, he saw the gift of it. As he slowed and watched, he had a renewed view of his wife. She had always been bursting with energy and enthusiasm and humor and so much creativity that sometimes it was overwhelming. Though older now, with silver highlights gleaming in her hair and laugh lines proclaiming to the world that she lived a joyful life, Helen hadn't slowed down. Now at home for his days, Kevin got to watch her do what she loved—pluck beauty from God's creation and create something others would cherish.

He loved that she did that. He loved that she could. And it amazed him that God had provided the means for it. For the second time in the space of a month, Kevin acknowledged, and this time fully embraced, the wonder in the fact that God had used his father to provide that gift. It felt like a long-overdue redemption of a relationship that had never been, because he could think on his dad with something other than darkness.

He could think on his father with gratitude. *A time to mend.*

This imposed rest also gave him the opportunity to oversee the surprise he had planned and had anticipated for a few years now. Thanks to the enthusiasm and skills of his children, it was all coming together better than he'd hoped.

On Christmas Eve-eve, Kevin wandered into the sunroom work space he'd built for Helen a decade ago and leaned against the large wooden table in the middle. He looked up and traced with his vision the carving he'd engraved in the exposed wooden beam in the ceiling. *Kevin loves Helen.*

Yes. Yes, he sure did.

Made him think of a conversation he'd had once with Buck Alexander many years back. Long before Buck became Brandon's father-in-law. Even well before Buck became the owner of a hunting sportsman empire.

"You sure work hard to make that woman happy," Buck had noted, more than a little jibing in his tone.

Kevin had shrugged and grinned. He could have told Buck that Helen deserved it—after all she'd put up with in their early years of marriage. She'd stayed when no one would have blamed her for leaving. That entitled her to some spoilage. Instead, he just caught Buck's eyes and held a firm stare. "Making my wife happy makes me happy. Isn't that how it should be?"

Buck had looked caught off. And then thoughtful. And then he'd just nodded. It didn't slip past Kevin's notice, however, that from that point forward, Buck had seemed to make a new effort in his marriage—one that previously, even from the distance of a casual friendship, had held the signs of tattered edges.

It also didn't slip past Kevin the last time he'd been with the Alexanders at their opulent place—when they'd gone to visit Brandon and Megan—that Buck and Anna seemed blissfully content with each other. Wealth and success had not damaged their marriage, and by all signs, Buck worked hard to make sure his wife was happy.

Kevin grinned. How did that adage go? Happy wife, happy life.

Just so.

Thinking of that, Kevin stood and peeked out the windows, his gaze searching the hillside beyond their backyard. Helen was out foraging—gathering the last bits of greenery for the garland she wanted to wrap the front deck handrails with before all of the children arrived that evening.

She had every surface covered in fresh greenery and holly. There were no fewer than five trees of various sizes scattered throughout the house, all decorated in what Helen called a *country chic style* and lit up with tiny yellow twinkle lights.

Nestled among the greenery strung over the fireplace mantel in this work space were two dozen LED candles.

Helen loved candles as much as she loved plants. She also loved Christmas and had been so looking forward to this one because all the boys and their families were coming. No small deal, as it had been a while since they'd all been in one place at one time. Not since . . . not since that Thanksgiving weekend when they'd all gathered at the lodge at Connor and Sadie's request.

Well, there had been Sadie's funeral. But who would ever count that? Not Kevin. Most assuredly not Helen.

This was a season of rejoicing. For the gathering of family and the gift of faith. For the birth of their Savior and the promise He brought with Him.

And for life. This beautiful, hard, gloriously rich life that Kevin hadn't dreamed possible.

Great is the Lord, and greatly to be praised!

At one time, his deepest longing was to know that someone valued him. Someone wanted him. That he would not forever be the virtually orphaned boy, the humiliated son of a drunk who would himself take on that ugly legacy.

God had given him more. Exceedingly, abundantly more than he'd ever imagined or dared to ask. And that lavish grace had started with Helen. The gift of his wife.

Tomorrow. Christmas Eve—the night before they celebrated the revelation of salvation to the world—Kevin would celebrate a different sort of redemption. The one that came with a marriage that had come as a result of reckless chaos and selfishness—but had been transformed into this blessing beyond measure. And by it and in it and through it, Kevin had been transformed.

His greatness is unsearchable. Praise God!

The redemption offered wasn't only a promise of a someday everlasting life—though that was stunning by itself. But not enough for the compassionate God who intervenes on ordinary, broken lives. Oh no! Not nearly enough. Instead, God took this lost, hopeless orphan and gave him a *life*! Here. Now. Full of love and hope and so much beauty that as he sat there, leaning again against that roughhewn table, Kevin could not stop the flow of his tears.

And that was good.

Because this was cleansing worship. A breaking of the old so the new could take hold. The final clutches of mistrust and resentment surrendered from the depths of his heart.

When it came to the memories he'd hated, now, at long last, he could finally and truly let his dad rest in peace.

He could once again rejoice in Dave's and George's lives. Lives that had unselfishly poured into his, though he deserved none of it.

And he could let Sadie go, embracing the miracle of healing in Connor's heart because his season of grieving had come to an end.

It was time to love again. Time to dance and rejoice and be glad.

And tomorrow . . .

Tomorrow would be lovely. Kevin could not wait to marry his bride all over again.

Outside, Helen straightened and waved the boughs of pine in her hand.

Ah, the kids were arriving—a little early, but who would mind that? Kevin clapped his hands together and rubbed his palms with eager delight.

Let the celebrating begin.

Helen burst through the French door that led into her sunroom, her grin already as wide as a Cheshire cat's. After dropping her armload of pine and fir, she spun to face Kevin, who was leaning casual as you please against the table. "They're here."

"I figured." He chuckled. "Since it looked like you were landing a plane out there." Reaching for her, he caught her at the waist by a fistful of her puffer coat and hauled her up close. "It's like you're excited or something."

She bit her lip. "It's Connor."

"Oh, well, if it's only Connor . . ."

She gave his shoulder a playful shove. "Stop." And then she sobered. Holding his dark, beautiful eyes, Helen gripped the material of his button-down shirt. "Kevin, we're okay with this, right?"

"With the kids coming home?" He winked and drew her in with both arms. "Only if they promise to leave after the party. At some point in the near future, I'm going to be healthy again, and you and I have some catching up to do . . ."

"Oh stop." She could feel the heat seeping into her chilly cheeks. "Sometimes you still act like a nineteen-year-old."

"Hmmm." He bent to catch her lips with his. "Who says nineteen-year-olds get to have all the fun?"

She leaned back. "I believe we said *none* of our nineteen-year-olds could have that kind of fun."

"Good thing they grew up and got married."

With both hands, she cupped his face. "Stay on track with me here."

Kevin chuckled. Teasing his wife had never, ever gotten old.

"I'm being serious. This is a serious question. It requires a serious answer."

"I prefer your serious questions to come with sexy nighties."

"Oh my goodness, Kevin Murphy!" She moved to give his laughing shoulders a light shake. "Never, ever tell the boys about that. Swear it right this second!"

He kept laughing. Worse, the sound of car doors shutting reported to them.

"Kevin."

"Okay, Helen. I promise I won't tell the boys how Brandon happened. Though at this point, I don't think—"

She slipped her fingers over his lips to shush him. "Listen, this *is* important. Lauren says Jade is terribly nervous about being here. About meeting us. So we're okay with this, right?" Gripping his collar, she leaned in. "We're *happy* about this."

Kevin leaned down and brushed her nose with his. "It's like you think I'm a scrooge all of the sudden."

Sighing, Helen went back to cradling his face. "Kevin, you've struggled with it. And I get it. But Connor is happy, and both Becca and Lauren approve. Please—"

He cut her off with a tender kiss as the sound of footfalls on the front steps reached their hearing. "I'm happy, Helen. I'm happy for Connor, and I'm happy to meet Jade and her kids, and if something more happens—" He cut off as if he knew something but wasn't going to say the rest. "I'm happy."

"Something more . . . like what?"

The front door clicked open.

Grinning, he kissed her forehead and stood up straight. "The kids cometh."

"But, Kev—"

He stepped away and called, "Connor! Reid!"

Helen scrambled after him, nearly forgetting that she still wore a stocking cap and likely had evergreen needles covering her head to toe. What *more* was going to happen? Surely Connor wouldn't propose here, would he? In front of this boisterous crowd, to a woman who apparently was shy and a little terrified to meet them all?

Her extraordinarily thoughtful, straight-as-an-arrow, do-the-right-thing, a-bit-on-the-dry-side son? Didn't seem like his style.

Then again, it might be terribly romantic.

But what if it embarrassed Jade? Or, for goodness' sake, she said no! Or worse, what if her kids objected? It could be a horrible disaster.

Oh heavens, what had Kevin meant?

Before she could unscramble her thoughts, let alone make them behave, she was in the front room and Connor was there, pulling her into his arms.

"Mom, the house looks amazing, as usual." Connor stepped back and turned toward the woman standing behind him in the doorway. With a tender smile and a move that shouted *protective* if ever she'd seen one, Connor curved an arm around her.

She was short and small framed. Her hair was straight and brown, and her eyes were the color of a rich coffee brew. Nothing about her was reminiscent of Sadie, and though Helen had been told that was the case, it surprised her.

"Mom. Dad." Connor looked down at the woman in his protective hold, his warm gaze nothing short of love. "This is Jade."

Helen felt a surrealness about that moment, though she couldn't define exactly why. She noticed Connor hadn't said Jade *Beck*, and she would have bet that had been intentional. To them, she would be Jade *Murphy*, and if Connor had his way, she would be so soon. By her soft glance up to him, Jade was in favor of that too.

And Helen felt . . . somehow stunned by it. Not unhappy. Not anything bad, just . . . stunned, and she couldn't say why.

Apparently, Kevin was not the only one to stumble with this life change.

"Jade." Kevin stepped forward, a smile in his voice as he reached out his hand. "It's good to finally meet you. Connor says you're wonderful."

A pretty pink blush flooded Jade's face as she took Kevin's hand. "He does?" She sounded breathless and shaken.

Kevin didn't shake Jade's hand. He pulled her into a hug. "Welcome."

Kevin left his greeting with an open ending. It could have been *welcome to the Murphy home*. Or *welcome to the Murphy family*. Helen had a feeling that he meant the latter. And she was proud of him, because he was being sincere.

Also, she noted that Matt was right about his dad and his girls, which meant Jade needn't be so nervous. Her husband was mush, and as far as Kevin was concerned, Jade was already one of them.

Years ago they had asked for *one* daughter. Now? Now they were well on their way to having loved eight of them.

Eight daughters!

How precious was that?

CHAPTER SIXTEEN

(in which the boys are back)

T he lovely aroma of a rich brew wafted in the kitchen, the pair of cof-
feepots Helen had started a few minutes after six now gurgling and
spitting. On top of her industrial-sized oven, three sheet pans of cinnamon
rolls waited under the cover of towels, ready to bake just as soon as the oven
was done preheating.

Already dressed in a pair of her favorite jeans and a soft gray sweater,
Helen had swept her hair into the French braid she commonly wore and
had donned her red pinstriped apron—the one that Kate and Jacob had
given her for Christmas last year. She hummed "Angels We Have Heard on
High" softly as she opened the refrigerator to retrieve the three large bags
of grapes she had waiting in there.

"Good morning, Mrs. Murphy," a timid voice said softly from behind.

A bit startled, but hoping it didn't show, Helen turned and found sweet
little Lily Beck on the other side of the large island that separated the
large kitchen from the even larger gathering space. Helen smiled. "Good
morning, Lily. You're up early."

She liked this girl, just as Reid had promised she would. Lily had a
sweetness that ran clear through, and she seemed to be an expert at nav-
igating situations that most would find awkward. Yesterday she had met
the Murphy crowd, as they trickled in, with a genuine smile and a way of
conversing that seemed beyond her sixteen years.

Lily had also aided her younger brother through it with a subtle grace that Helen only noticed because Connor had confided to her before they came that Kellen didn't do well with change and really struggled with crowds. Having that information, Helen had watched the younger Beck, praying for him, as this new situation must be hard. The boy stuck by Lily and Reid, and Lily gave him more than a few encouraging looks and made sure she didn't wander off without him unless Reid was nearby.

The kids were good together. They were already a close crew—they'd be a lovely family, and Helen had silently thanked God last night that He'd so kindly put them together.

And Lily . . . was charming. *Love at first sight.* The thought—an echo of what she'd thought of all of her children and grandchildren—warmed her heart and made her smile grow as she leaned on the counter across from her newest family acquisition. "Did you sleep okay?"

A light blush touched Lily's cheeks as she shrugged. "Mom was a bit restless. New places are like that."

Compassion flooded Helen's heart. "I'm sure nerves likely played a role. We're quite a bunch to take in all at once."

"Yeah." Lily looked at her hands. "She's nervous." With a daring courage, Lily met Helen's eyes. "We all are, to be honest."

Ah. A kind one with courageous honesty. Helen pushed off the counter and circled round until she was at Lily's side. She dropped an arm around the girl's shoulder and squeezed. "I can understand that. Maybe it doesn't help, but I'm sure glad you're here."

Lily leaned in briefly. "It helps. Thank you."

"Little Isaac sure thought you're the cat's meow." Helen laughed as she moved back toward the oven, replaying how three-year-old Isaac had fallen instantly in love with Lily, snuggling on her lap when she sat next to Reid and insisting that she be the one to carry him off to bed when it was time to say good night.

"He's a cutie."

"He's a mini-Brayden, all enchanting and adorable. Audrey will have her hands full, especially if this next baby is anything of the same. Which is likely, as the Murphy charm runs deep."

Lily giggled and made her way toward the sink. "Can I help you with anything?"

Helen stood, having slid the last of the three pans into the oven. "That's kind of you, but you certainly don't have to do anything."

"I'd like to help, if you have anything."

Placing her hands on her hips, she let her fingers drumroll against her sides as she thought. "I was just going to wash up the grapes. Would you mind doing that?"

"That would be easy." Lily started in right away, and Helen set a pair of scissors and a large bowl beside the sink where she worked.

"Reid says you're quite a basketball player."

A fresh flush of pink brushed her cheeks. "I like playing ball. It's nice to have Reid around too. He pushes me to be better. And Connor. It's really fun when we all play together. Even mom comes out—and she's good at basketball."

"Did you learn how to play from her?"

Lily shrugged. "She taught me how to shoot, how to dribble. When I was little, we'd go to the park and play some. But that stopped for a while—she was too busy, and life was just . . . different." A sadness touched Lily's tone.

Helen wondered if that *different* had to do with the divorce. It didn't seem appropriate to ask though.

For several moments the pair fell into silent work. So many questions marched through Helen's mind. How did Lily feel about her dad? Were they close? Was the divorce hard? Was it hard to see Connor step into a place with her mom that she felt didn't belong to him? Or was she okay with everything between Connor and Jade? Helen found her heart throbbing with worry for this precious girl she'd already taken in as one of her own.

"Mrs. Murphy?"

Helen wanted to tell her to call her Gran, but perhaps that wasn't okay right then. "Yes, dear Lily?"

"Connor is really great." Full-on red flooded her face. "I just wanted you to know that. For a long time, I thought men were . . . selfish. Kind of mean, and when my mom and dad divorced, I had honestly hoped that she wouldn't find anyone else, because I didn't think—" Lily cut off her thoughts and then straightened her shoulders. "Anyway, I'm glad to find out I was wrong. I'm super thankful for Connor and Reid."

Big eyes full of tenderness met Helen's, and then Lily finished with the best thing Helen could imagine. "We love them."

Helen blinked back the heat in her eyes and gathered Lily in a bear hug. "I'm glad to know that, Lily." She stepped back and held the girl by her shoulders. "And if Connor is ever mean or selfish, you'd better come straight to me about it."

Lily chuckled and shook her head. "I can't imagine that he ever would be. Even when he was a grumpy bear when we first moved to the lake, he wasn't anything like . . ."

Though Lily's voice trailed off, Helen could fill in the rest. And she wanted to hunt down the man who had fathered this sweet girl and give him a piece of her mind and maybe the backside of her wooden spoon. Instead, she focused on the first bit of that statement.

"Connor was a bear, was he?"

"Don't worry—it didn't last long. I think he liked my mom but didn't want to. That's what Reid says, anyway."

Huh. She'd been left out of entirely too much of this story. "I might just need to have a chat with my son."

Lily turned laughing eyes toward Helen. "They worked it out. Thanks to Reid and me."

Brows lifting, Helen stopped stirring the orange juice she'd been mixing from concentrate and leaned in. "What did you do?"

Biting her lip, Lily leaned in close and whispered, "We just made sure that they had plenty of opportunities to get to know each other."

"Apparently it worked, hmm?"

"What are we whispering about in here, girls?"

In unison, Helen and Lily both stood straight and whipped around at the sound of Kevin's voice. "Don't be sneaking around, Kevin Murphy."

Kevin kept coming until he was close enough to drop an arm around each girls' shoulders. He leaned down and whispered, "What are we discussing?"

Helen glanced at Lily, playful conspiracy arching her brows. "The fact that your son was a bear to Jade when she first moved to the lake, but Lily and Reid took care of it," she whispered.

"Ah." Kevin grinned at Lily. "I heard you parent-trapped them."

Lily beamed.

"Good job." Kevin winked and then stood straight.

Lily stepped back, and her expression shifted. "Wait! It's your anniversary today, right?"

Kevin tightened his arm around Helen, and Helen leaned her head into his chest. "It is," she said. "How did you know that."

"Connor told us." Her eyes grew wide. "Oh I'm sorry! I should have said it first thing. Happy anniversary."

"Thank you, Lily." Kevin kissed the top of Helen's head. "Happy anniversary, love."

"You too." Helen looked up at him and smiled.

Kevin turned his attention back to Lily. "I like this kid. I think we should keep her."

Her grin grew wider, and she looked at Lily again and gripped her hand. "I very much agree."

Lily didn't respond with words, but the joy and hope brimming in her eyes was more than enough.

Christmas was looking lovely all the way around.

The sun shone warm for a Christmas Eve morning, and the family trickled onto the back southern-facing deck as the fog burned away. Dressed in thick hoodies, feet in socks and slippers, the adults found their way to a spot near the railing, each holding a plate of warm cinnamon rolls and a mug of something steamy and delicious.

"The frost on the pines looks magical," Audrey said wistfully.

"Does it make you homesick?" Megan asked. "Because home is definitely sick for you."

Brayden stood behind Audrey and wrapped one strong arm around her so that she could lean back against him. Covering her growing baby bump, Audrey sighed. "Not too homesick usually. I think we're too busy. But this baby . . ." She made a face that said the rest. The nausea hadn't gone away, despite being five months in.

"Well, I think Brayden needs to hurry up and be a real doctor so you can come home." Megan turned her sassy expression to Brayden. "I still haven't forgiven you, by the way."

"I know." Brayden hung his head in mock shame. "I will bring her back, I promise."

Helen wasn't sure about all that had passed between Brandon and Megan and Brayden and Audrey, other than that Megan and Audrey had always been close—and somehow Brayden had turned things awry for a time. But she was relieved to see a playful banter between them.

She also didn't miss the way Megan had eyed Audrey's baby bump with a longing look, or the brief moment when she'd surreptitiously covered her own womb with her palm. Perhaps now, after five years of marriage, it was time. A would-be grandmother could hope. But she wouldn't say anything. Especially knowing how much Jacob and Kate had struggled with several miscarriages. One just never knew, and Helen didn't want to bring up anything that would be hurtful.

Jackson stood up from his leaning position on the rail and raised his mug. "I'm in for another. Anyone else want a refill?"

Jacob passed his mug and his empty plate to Jackson. "No on the roll—just thought you'd play busboy." He tipped a half grin. "But I'll take more coffee."

"As you wish. Snob." Jackson elbowed Jacob, and both men chuckled.

Helen's heart buoyed at their interaction. There had been a time when those two boys couldn't hold a civil conversation—forget any sort of bantering. Things had been so much better between that pair for the past few years. Amazing what a little bit of humility and honesty and forgiveness could do. Not to mention her butting out.

Praise God, He does work miracles.

Turning toward Connor and Jade, who stood side by side on the opposite part of the deck, Jackson looked at the newest part of the group. "How about you, Jade? Surely you're going to need more than one cup of coffee to survive this rowdy bunch."

The woman gave him a small smile. "I'd take a refill. Thank you."

"You're not going to offer to get me one?" Connor said wryly.

"You've got legs." Jackson turned toward a different brother. "Tyler though. I'd gladly help you out, brother."

Tyler shoved Jackson's shoulder as he laughed. "Thanks. I've also got legs. Can outclimb you any day of the week, and I can probably outrun you these days too."

Patting his gut, which was a little more than it had been ten years ago when he'd been bound and determined to qualify for the Boston Marathon, Jackson feigned an injured look. "What are you saying?"

"I'm saying the Boston is likely in your rearview mirror."

"Huh." Jackson scowled. Then he turned to head inside but paused just long enough to wink in Jade's direction.

Jade looked . . . baffled. Poor girl. Likely this sounded awful to her—especially if her ex-husband was, as Helen could guess after the conversation with Lily that morning, an unkind man. Hopefully, her ornery sons weren't scaring Jade off.

"He's teasing," Helen said. "They're all teasing."

"I told you they were a bunch of ruffians and thugs." Lauren smiled and gripped Jade's hands.

"Not even close." Matt draped his arm around his wife. "We're all a bunch of overgrown teddy bears. Just ask Megan. She's stuck with the worst of us, and he's not so bad."

Megan giggled, and Brandon scowled, right up until he looked down at his wife, at which point he turned to complete mush. Just like his dad. "Am I the worst?"

"I think I remember saying that to you at some point," Megan said. "And I wasn't just talking about the Murphy men."

"Here we are though. Mr. and Mrs."

"Weird." Megan lifted to her toes and kissed Brandon's cheek. "But I'll keep you."

From inside the house, Jackson called back, "Tyler, I'm gonna call you out on that, so you'd better find yourself a running leg, and then you'd better start training."

"Great. Thanks, Ty." Kenzie rolled her eyes. "Now he's back to marathons again." She looked at Becca. "Prepare yourself. The early morning runs. The obsession with times. And the worst part, the laundry. You can't wash that kind of stink out."

"I forbid it." Becca held a stern look on Tyler.

"Do you now?"

A tiny grin peeked from the corner of her mouth.

Tyler smiled like a champion. "We'll negotiate later."

The blush on Becca's face tattled on exactly what Tyler meant. Also just like his father.

Jackson passed back through the doors, Reid right behind him. Both carried mugs of fresh coffee. Reid handed one cup to Jade and the other to his dad. Connor traded his empty mug for the fresh one and then patted Reid's shoulders. "Here's a good one. Way to show your uncle how it's done, son."

Reid grinned and walked away. Helen eyed him as he moved, because there was a glint in that kid's eye—not one that was common for that particular boy.

They chatted about nothing in particular, enjoying the frosty view and the piney mountain air for several minutes before Connor discovered what his son had been up to.

Connor lifted his mug to take a drink and stopped with a jerk. "What the—" He looked straight at Reid, brows pulled down, and then at Jackson. "What did you do?"

"What is it?" Jade took the mug and looked at the contents. And then shrieked while flinging it away.

A full mug of fresh coffee went flying . . . right in Connor's face.

"Oh my gosh! Connor. I'm so sorry!" Jade set her own mug on the deck rail and covered her mouth with both hands.

Using the sleeve of his black sweatshirt, Connor wiped his dripping wet face. Once his eyes were clear, he picked the large plastic spider that was now hanging from one of the pull strings of his hoodie, held it out, and pinned a glare on Jackson. He shook his head, his expression dark. And then . . . then he burst out laughing.

Jackson lifted his mug toward Reid, a silent salute to their prank, and the rest of the Murphys erupted with laughter as well.

"You are not allowed to corrupt my son," Connor said between chuckles. He pulled Jade in close against him and then looked at Reid. "I can't believe you would be in on this. You scared Jade to death."

Reid crossed his arms and leaned against the house, his expression smug as you please. "You did that, Dad. Not me. But the coffee in your face was pretty epic. We didn't plan that part." Then he studied Jade for a moment, and his smirk sobered. "You're not mad, right, Jade? I wasn't aiming for—"

Jade pulled away from Connor and looked at Reid, humor brimming in her eyes as she laughed silently. "Not mad at all. That was, as you said, epic. Connor only warned me about Jackson."

Jackson puffed out his chest. "The master is *still* in the house. Well done, my young apprentice. Next we'll cover all the amazingly disgusting things you can do with a candy bar."

A collective groan lifted from the group.

"Well . . ." Megan smiled, stepped toward Jade, and gripped her arm. "You know what they say—the couple who can stay together through coffee in the face will stay together through anything."

"Who says that?" Audrey gave her friend a *you're ridiculous* look. "No one says that, Meg."

"Megan does," Brandon deadpanned. "It makes her feel better about it."

Still grinning, Jade turned to Brandon, clearly no longer intimidated by the Murphy men. "About what?"

"About tossing coffee in my face." Brandon tipped his mug to his lips, as if that little announcement was the stuff of everyday occurrences.

"What?" Audrey squealed. "You didn't."

"I absolutely did." Megan lifted her chin and pinned her sassy look on her husband. "And he absolutely deserved it. I'm still not sorry. And also, you laughed."

"Did not." The way the corner of Brandon's mouth poked upward proclaimed the opposite.

Helen stepped back while the kids continued their banter, thoroughly amused to watch her most serious son and his slightly silly wife balance each other out. They were adorable. All of them, actually.

A pair of strong arms slipped around her. Sighing, she leaned back as Kevin tugged her in close. "Quite a crowd we have gathered here, beautiful."

"Yes it is," she said. "To think we get to claim them."

"Not bad for a pair of lost kids who had no idea what they were getting into, hmm?"

"Not bad at all." She tipped her face up to find his turned down to her. The love in his eyes warmed her clean through, and she moved to kiss his lips. "I'd do it all again. Hands down, no reserve. I'd say yes to you again in a heartbeat."

"Would you?" He brushed her nose with his. "I might just hold you to that one of these days."

"We go every time we come. I'd like for you to come. It's really okay."

Helen heard Connor's low voice drifting from the hallway and knew she'd stumbled into a private conversation. Even so, she paused.

"I feel like that would be terribly invasive," Jade whispered back. "Maybe the kids and I will just . . . I don't know what. We'll stay here. It might be good for Kellen to take a bit of a time-out anyway. We both know what would happen if he got too overwhelmed."

"Kellen is having fun." A mild rebuke carried in Connor's voice, and then it softened again. "They would like to meet you, Jade. I'm sure of it."

Ah. The Allens.

Helen's heart squeezed for the difficult place Jade must feel she was in. Connor and Reid always visited Sadie's parents when they were in town. On more than one occasion, Reid would stay with them—as that had been the normal place all three had stayed when Sadie was still alive. Helen had little doubt, in fact, that if it was just Connor and Reid on this trip and the Allens were still in their old home rather than the retirement village in town, the pair would still stay with them. And that would have been perfectly okay, because Reid was all Samuel and Eleanor had left of Sadie. That was sacred to Connor. It was sacred to all of them.

Such hard things.

Helen shut her eyes and lifted a quick prayer for Connor and Jade, as well as for the Allens. But especially for Jade. What a whirlwind holiday this was turning out to be for her. So much so that part of Helen hoped that Connor *wouldn't* propose.

Not in front of everyone, son, she silently pressed to him.

Then Helen sent up a quick prayer for guidance—and grace from both Connor and Jade as she inserted herself into a conversation in which she didn't belong.

Clutching her hands, she strode forward anyway. "I'm sorry."

Connor looked up, and Jade turned to face her. By the wide look in her brown eyes, the younger woman was terribly uncomfortable.

Helen reached for her hand and squeezed it. "Forgive me for being a nosy mom. I just overheard part of your conversation."

Connor furrowed his brow and aimed dark eyes on her. Helen felt keenly her son's irritation. Even so, she plunged ahead.

"I am certain, Jade, that Samuel and Eleanor Allen would like to meet you. At some point, anyway." She looked up at Connor and held a meaningful *mom* stare on him. "But I can also understand why you wouldn't be ready for that on this trip. So I just thought I'd tell you that Kevin and I are taking the rest of the grands to the sledding hill for a few hours. We'd love it if you and Lily and Kellen came with us." Helen gave Jade a small grin she hoped was only encouraging and then glanced again at her son. "I'm done interfering now. Carry on."

Connor's frown relaxed, and a hint of gratitude even filtered into his gaze as he nodded. Turning, Helen scurried away, leaving the awkward silence at her back.

"Go!" Little Isaac waved his hands as he sat in Lily's lap, the pair of them folded onto a disk sled. Brayden gave them a hardy shove, and the air was rent with a three-year-old's delighted squeal.

"I'm beating you!" Helene, Fiona's little sister, yelled, though she was not. Alone on her disk on another path beside them, she trailed behind a good five feet.

At the bottom the older kids waved and cheered. Bobbie Joy bounced up and down, her ginger curls swinging from beneath her teal stocking cap. Beside her, Kellen also cheered. Helen smiled at that budding friendship. It seemed like a confirmation, a nod from heaven, that this shift in Connor's life was blessed by God.

"You're not winning, Helene!" Fiona, always the big sister and usually the boss, corrected from her spot on the other side of Bobbie Joy.

Helen chuckled as she watched from the bench near the pond. She scanned the area around the pond, simultaneously checking to make sure the kids stayed off the unstable ice and looking for the girls' mothers, because likely Lauren was due a break from her youngest little storm cloud. Hopefully, baby Ainsley would outgrow her clingy neediness soon.

The pond was clear, but though she spotted Megan and Audrey chatting and laughing with Jade, and Becca and Kate at the top of the hill with Jackson and Jacob, distributing turns on sleds with as much fairness as possible, she didn't spot Lauren and Kenzie. Come to think of it, where was Matt, Tyler, and Brandon?

Helen turned to Kevin, who begrudgingly sat at her side when he wanted to go and wrestle in the snow with some grandkids. "We're missing some."

"What's that?"

"We're missing some kids."

Using his gloved hand, Kevin counted grandchildren. "Nope. All there but Reid, and he's with his dad."

"No, not grandchildren. *Our* kids. We're missing five of them."

"Huh." Kevin shrugged. "Must have gotten tired."

"Tyler? Lauren?" Helen frowned at him. "Too tired for this kind of fun? When have you ever witnessed that?"

Watching the activity on the hill, Kevin merely shrugged again. But something tugged on his lips. Something . . . suspicious.

Helen leaned in closer. "What are you up to, mister? First you tell me I *must* get out of the kitchen. Then you insist that the kids *must* go sledding. Now you are trying to tell me two of the most energetic people on the planet are tired and they somehow convinced three others to go back with them for a group nap?"

"I didn't say that."

Helen crossed her arms. "Tell."

Amused eyes turned on her, and Kevin straightened her stocking cap. "My dear wife, some things you must simply trust me with."

"But what is going on?"

He kissed her forehead and then sat back and laughed.

CHAPTER SEVENTEEN

(in which marriage is holy)

"**M**ama Helen, you have to come with us."

Rather than question Kenzie, who along with Lauren and Becca had intercepted her path up the driveway and to the house, Helen turned her suspicious gaze onto the man who held her hand. "What is going on here?"

As he had up at the sledding hill, Kevin just chuckled. "You'll see." He turned her by the shoulders and gave her backside a sassy little pat. "Do as you're told."

Helen flung a mildly irritated look at the man over her shoulder a breath before she was dragged by both arms, one tugged by Becca and the other by Kenzie.

"It's a fun surprise, Mama." Lauren beamed as she walked backward so she could face Helen. "I promise you'll like it."

Forcing a mocked scowl, Helen met the jolly young woman's eyes with her own. "*I* do the surprises at Christmas."

"It's not Christmas," Becca sassed.

"But—" Helen nearly complained about the Christmas Eve soup that she needed to check on. And there were rolls that needed to go into the oven, and she wanted to see that the apple and cherry pies she'd baked were cooling properly. And oh! She still needed to whip the cream to go with those pastries. But realization struck.

It was their anniversary.

Normally, the day that marked another year beyond their vows was celebrated with a simple *happy anniversary, honey*. Choosing to marry on Christmas Eve sort of did that, but neither she nor Kevin had ever really minded. Their marriage was something they both cherished every day, worked at every day. One day wasn't a make-it-or-break-it kind of deal.

But this . . . this was their *fortieth* anniversary. Perhaps that was a big deal.

Stumbling through the ankle-deep snow after her daughters-in-love, a giddy girlish sort of sensation bubbled in her middle. Kevin had planned something special, and he'd recruited the kids to see it through.

"Oh no, she's guessed it, I think." Kenzie dropped Helen's hand, as they had to shift into single file onto the path that would take them to the cabin. For the time, Brandon and Megan and Brayden and Audrey were staying there, so it didn't make sense that these three girls were leading Helen that direction.

Except whatever Kevin had planned was something really special.

"What have you guessed?" Becca glanced backward with a mischievous grin.

"I have no idea. But I'm sure I'll like it."

"You're going to love it!" Lauren clapped her hands and squealed. Not really a Lauren-esque sort of thing to do, except she did have a daughter named Fiona who oozed drama like it was her lifeblood.

"Does it involve your cupcakes, Bec?"

The woman ahead of her shrugged. "I'm sworn to secrecy."

"Does it involve your floral work, Kenz?"

"I would die before I sold out Daddy Murph's surprise."

Lauren held up a hand to stall Helen's next question. "It involves a hat. That's all I'm saying."

A hat? Helen adjusted the stocking cap on her head. Why on earth would Kevin's surprise involve a hat?

The girls marched Helen straight to the cabin and through that short front door, and the moment she was inside, they stripped her of her outdoor winter gear.

"I feel like I'm involved with a gang of thieves here. Do I get to keep my clothes on?"

"Nope." Shaking out Helen's puffer coat, Lauren laughed and then pointed to the door on the right, one of two tiny bedrooms in this small space. "But you can have the dignity of changing yourself. Your evening attire is in there."

Trying not to giggle while the girls worked ever so hard at not beaming, Helen eyed them with all the bits of motherly disapproval she could muster. It wasn't much and she knew it. Then she followed the pointing fingers and took herself into that small bedroom she and Kevin had shared for several years.

One glance at the bed, and her breath caught. Laid out for her was a lovely vintage-style champagne dress embroidered with delicate white flourishes, the tiny beadwork stitched in. It was exactly her size and exactly a style she would have picked for herself at this stage in life. Beside it was a pair of white elbow-length satin gloves to match. And to the side lay the hat.

The hat. How had she forgotten about the hat she'd worn rather than a veil? It'd been ever so important to her, though she could not for the life of her say why. And Kevin . . .

It had been one of the few details he remembered about their wedding day. That was a bittersweet truth that he'd confessed to her a half a dozen years into their marriage. He'd told her that he'd focused on the brim of that hat as she'd walked down the aisle, breathlessly anticipating when she would look up at him. And because of that, Helen now understood what he'd been up to.

Today, they would do it all over again.

She'd never really considered a vow renewal. Truthfully, it hadn't seemed like an important thing to think about. But as it clearly was something that had pressed on Kevin's heart, hers melted into it.

"Mama Helen?" Becca spoke softly from the doorframe.

Helen turned. Suddenly she was aware that a sheen of tears threatened to spill from her eyes. She blinked them back and smiled at the trio of girls watching her.

"It's lovely."

"Daddy Murph asked Kate to pick it out—but she insisted he approve it." Kenzie said. "And he wanted the hat."

"Yes." Helen glanced back at that accessory. It had held him in place at the front of the church that day when every frightened instinct he'd had screamed for him to bolt. "He would."

Lauren's brows rose at that, but she didn't ask. "Kate will be here in a few minutes to do hair and makeup. Then your ride arrives in forty."

"My ride?" They hadn't maintained the driveway to the front of the cabin. When the kids used it, they did so with a beast of a four-wheel drive—usually Brandon's old truck. The one that Megan swore she'd put into the lake someday when he wasn't looking. Helen pictured herself climbing into that thing wearing her new beautiful dress.

Ew. She'd rather walk the half mile, thank you very much. Also, perhaps it was time she went into cahoots with Megan on the truck-sinking plan. It was well past its prime and needed an irreversible burial.

"We walked here just fine—"

Yet again Lauren held a hand up. "You'll see. And you'll love it."

Thirty-eight minutes later, Helen felt elegant in her new 1920s-style dress. The V-neck and drop waist were a flattering cut, and the delicate patterns worked into the shiny fabric added just enough glam to make it special, but not over the top. Kate had swept Helen's hair back in a loose, flat braid that she had wrapped at her neck, creating an elegant, bohemian style that easily accommodated the 1980s wedding hat.

She was a style mashup of decades and loved it.

Kate pushed the final pins that would secure the hat. "That does it." Her blue eyes danced as she smiled at Helen in the mirror. "You're stunning."

Helen stood, and the girls—now four of them in the cabin with her—oohed and ahhed.

"I assume you have a groom for me somewhere." Helen winked.

Before anyone could answer, the sound of men clamoring and talking loudly outside cut in. None of them, however, were Kevin. The door burst open, and there stood Matt, Jacob, and Jackson. All dressed in suit pants, snow boots, and winter coats, and all wearing a red-plaid fur-lined trapper hat. Helen laughed at the sight.

"Oh, this keeps getting better!" She clapped her hands. "What are we doing now?"

Jackson bowed and swept an arm toward the door. "Your sled awaits."

"My sled? Are there dogs?"

"Ruff," Jackson deadpanned.

"Aha. Now I know why God gave me sons!" Helen patted Jackson's face as she moved toward the door.

Kate stopped her from exiting, with one hand on her exposed upper arm. "One more surprise. This one is from the boys."

"Yikes. I don't know about that . . ."

"I'll take it if you don't want it," Jackson said.

Kenzie snorted. "I'd like to see you in it. Along with that hat. We'll take pictures and post them."

"You're on." Jackson crossed his arms.

"Oh stop." Kate waved Jackson toward the door. "Everyone is waiting." Then she retrieved a long garment bag from behind the second bedroom door. From that she pulled a wrap trimmed in faux sable fur.

"Ohhh . . ." Helen breathed as Kate draped the thick, soft garment around her shoulders. She looked at the men still lingering at the door. "It's lovely."

Jacob glanced at his wife, and his expression was all soft appreciation. Kate must have picked this out as well. Then he bent to kiss Helen's cheek. "Merry Christmas, Mom."

Helen stepped into his embrace, chilly though it was, and then moved to hug the other two sons in the room.

Matt hooked an arm around her and guided her to the door. "No mushy stuff, now. We have things to do."

The group filed out the door, and Helen laughed at the sled for one waiting outside. "Who did this?"

"Ty, mostly," Matt said.

"Such a big deal you all are making."

"Dad's orders." Jackson swept his arm toward the single seat and bowed. "And now, my lady, if you'll make yourself comfortable . . ."

Helen did as she was told, and the boys took their places—two at the thick ropes at the front, and one at the back.

"Mush!" Helen called, and off they went.

Helen laughed the whole way there.

"Do you approve?" Kenzie looked at Kevin with hopeful eyes.

They'd cleared away the large worktable Helen used in the sunroom, giving open access to the stone fireplace on the far side of the room. Twinkle lights draped from the ceiling, creating a cozy tent ambiance, and a warm fire danced in the belly of the stone. The thick, roughhewn mantel was covered in greenery and lit LED candles.

It was exactly as Helen would want it, Kevin was certain. And if she were to plan her wedding now, he felt sure that this would be her dream. He couldn't wait for her to have it.

Emotion stirring in his chest, Kevin nodded and hugged her. "It's perfect. She'll love it."

"They're here." Brandon straightened his dark suit coat and squeezed Kevin's shoulder. "Are you ready?"

"Absolutely." Kevin beamed and then lifted his brows at his son. "The real question is, are you?"

Brandon cleared his throat and answered with a half a grin. He was nervous—this would be his first.

A finger of quivering anticipation drew through Kevin's middle. Whether it was to see his bride's reaction to this surprise or on behalf of Brandon's nerves, Kevin wasn't sure, but either way it sent a chain of shivers as the clamoring of feet pounded up the front steps and then through the front door.

Then a hush settled over the room. The kids and grandchildren—all thirty-plus of them—wandered quietly to take their places. Nearest Kevin at the front of where the ceremony was to take place, Elizabeth Clayton stood from the chair they'd placed for her. Samuel and Eleanor Allen remained seated because standing for any length had become too much. Mixed in with Brayden and a few grandchildren—greats to them—Helen's parents also stood. This time genuine approval filled their whole expressions. Standing beside Megan, Buck and Anna Alexander beamed as they watched for the bride.

This time, this redo . . . it was perfect.

Kevin leaned toward Brandon, who was now standing in front of the fireplace, and whispered, "Ready or not, here we go."

The words were barely off his lips when the sight of Helen and that silly, wonderful hat stole his full attention. She carried a bouquet of white daffodils—some of her favorite flowers, and stems that were hard to come by this time of year. This time Helen did not make him wait in agony to meet his gaze. Those blue eyes searched his out and once latched, held.

Kevin's heart clutched and breath caught, and everything around faded to an inconsequential haze.

Forty years. Years full of laughter and tears, struggles and ease. Forty years with the same lovely woman, and yet simply the sight of her seized his heart and filled him with overflowing joy and love.

This time Helen did not look at the floor when she stepped toward him, Matt her escort. Then she was there, handing Kenzie that bouquet and then slipping her hand into his. Her blue eyes brimmed with tenderness and—dare he claim so?—adoration.

It was entirely mutual. Kevin tugged her closer and leaned to brush a kiss against her cheek. "You're lovely, Helen."

"This is a lovely surprise," she whispered back.

In front of them, as well as the whole gathering, Brandon cleared his throat. "Dearly beloved, we are gathered together today in the sight of—"

"Wait." Helen stepped back and turned a quizzical look on their son. "Are you allowed to do this?"

Brandon scowled. "Would you prefer someone else?"

"No. I mean, is it legal?"

His folded brows lifted into amusement, and he chuckled. "Was it not legal before?"

"Great," Jackson grumbled playfully behind them. "Turns out our parents weren't married, boys. What else don't we know?"

An entertaining blush seeped into Helen's cheeks and spread to the roots of her hair. "That's not what I said." She looked up at Kevin as if to say, *Deal with your sons.*

Kevin laughed. "Brandon, show your mother the papers."

With a gleam of pride, Brandon dug into the inside pocket of his suit jacket and produced a folded certificate declaring that he was an ordained minister, legally recognized in the state of California.

Still blushing, Helen beamed and hugged Brandon. "Congratulations, Brandon! That's thrilling!"

"May I continue?" Brandon tugged himself straight again, feigning the normal seriousness of his nature.

"Please do." Helen settled back into place, taking Kevin's hands.

He cleared his throat again. "To witness the recommitment of vows between these two special people. Dad. Mom." Brandon looked at each individually, and deep emotion filled his gaze. "We've watched you go through the years with laughter and tears. We've witnessed you fight, and disgustingly, we've witnessed you kiss." He paused, made a face, and then switched back to serious mode. "I think every one of us boys would say that because of you, we work hard to make a good marriage."

Whispers of *yes* and *amen* drifted through the room.

"So it is our joy and honor to be with you here today, on your fortieth anniversary, and to celebrate a renewal of your vows." Brandon paused and then nodded to Kevin. "Dad, I think you wanted to say something?"

Kevin drew in a breath. He'd written the things he wanted to say—the little sheet was in his coat pocket. But as he focused on the woman he loved, he found he didn't need it.

"Helen, my beloved. Forty years ago I married you as a frightened young man who saw you as my way out. Out of loneliness. Out of a life I hated. You were my way into being someone somebody wanted. And it was also the way out of trouble. Forty years ago on our wedding day, I knew I was a coward, and I also knew I wasn't what you deserved. Truth be told, I was terrified, and the only way I made it through the ceremony was by the aid of strong drink.

"There is no way to tell you how much I have regretted that." Kevin had to pause to swallow the lump in his throat.

"So today I want to stand here before you as a sober man. One who is more concerned with being who I should be for you, and before God, than having you fill a void that only proved to take us both into a dark place. I want to promise you the next forty years from my heart. When I say for better or for worse, I mean it—but not because my drinking is bound to make it for worse. I will work every day so that, as far as it is in my power, your life will be better with me. When I say for richer or for poorer, I mean it—but I also know with absolute certainty that with you at my side, I am always richer, no matter what the bank says."

He bent, touching his forehead to hers. "You have my respect. My fidelity. And all of my love." Lifting her hands to his chest, he pulled in another breath. "So today, will you marry me all over again?"

As a beautiful peace draped over them, the room held for one breathless, memorable moment.

With tears slipping onto her cheeks, Helen laughed softly. "I will."

Unexpected relief washed through him, and Kevin pulled her into an embrace.

"I don't know what I'm doing up here," Brandon deadpanned. "You're doing just fine on your own, Dad."

Kevin straightened and stepped back, reclaiming Helen's hands. "Make it official, son."

A deep chuckle left Brandon's throat, and then he began. "Mom"—he winked—"will you continue to have Dad as your husband and continue to live in this marriage? Will you continue to love him, to faithfully remain with him in all times and circumstances, good and bad, forsaking all others, until death?"

"I will," Helen sputtered.

Kevin felt a tear leak from the corner of his eye, but he didn't bother to brush it away.

"Dad, will you continue to have Mom as your wife and continue to live in this marriage? Do you reaffirm your constant love for her and promise to be her comfort, her confidant, her champion, and her best friend? Will you remain faithful come what may, forsaking all others, until death?"

That pesky lump had grown. Kevin swallowed it back again. "With all my heart, I will."

Another pause stretched, and a few sniffles sounded through the otherwise hushed room. One from Brandon before he continued.

"As officiant, it is my duty to remind you, and all in hearing who have also taken these sacred vows at some point, that these commitments are not to be taken lightly. Our God has declared that what He has joined together, no man is to tear apart. As He loves, we are to love. As he sacrifices, so do we. As He is faithful to us, we are to be faithful to each other. Marriage is holy, set apart from all other relationships. It is to be kept holy. Will we all enter that vow, reminding one another of it when the time is necessary for it?"

The entire gathering of adults responded, "We will."

Brandon nodded, and joy replaced the seriousness of his expression. "Mom, Dad, as you have proclaimed your ongoing love before the witness of this family, and have renewed your commitment in marriage, it is my pleasure to announce that you are ... still ... married." He turned a warning look onto Kevin. "Without being gross about it, Dad, you can kiss your bride."

"Oh, you know I'm gonna." Kevin framed Helen's face and found her lips with his own.

The groans came in quick order, but that only made him and Helen laugh as they continued to kiss.

After all, they were married. They could kiss for as long as they wanted.

CHAPTER EIGHTEEN

(in which Christmas is lovely)

H elen sipped on her hot white chocolate—a gift made by the sweet Jade Beck—and smiled. With plates full of apple cinnamon French toast and mugs of something hot and delicious, her grown children gathered in chairs made into a wide circle in the large gathering space of their home. In the background, a strings group played "The First Noel" from Helen's Spotify Christmas playlist. A fire crackled cheerfully from the sunroom fireplace, and the large tree in the corner of the front room twinkled with all of its merry might.

The grandchildren—all fifteen of them!—milled from parents to kitchen to Christmas tree and everywhere else, all wearing the matching gray-and-white snowflake jammies and hats that they'd opened the night before.

Ah . . . the evening before. What a beautiful, emotional, absolutely wonderful evening it had been. After the vow renewal ceremony, the daughters went straight to work, dishing soup and pie and cleaning up messes as they went. Becca had presented Kevin and Helen with a beautiful little anniversary cake, which they ceremoniously cut and then the grandchildren devoured.

And sweet little Mack, Jackson and Kenzie's five-year-old son, had shyly tugged on Helen's hand. "Grans?" he whispered.

"Yes, my little Mack-truck."

"You look very pretty."

Helen hugged him. "Thank you, sweet boy!"

He grinned—a smile that, save Jackson's scar on his lip—was exactly his father's. All charming boy about to go for what he wanted. Helen braced herself.

"Do we still get Eve presents?" His little fingers twisted together while he asked.

Laughing, Helen had tucked him in close. "Absolutely! They're the silver packages under the medium tree." She pointed to the Christmas tree she meant—the one closest to the dining table. "Go get Reid and Lily and see if they'll help you hand them out."

Mack had clapped and then on a run, called, "Reid! It's time for Eve presents!"

Certainly no one could have been surprised by the matching Christmas pj's—she did it all the time. But they still loved them.

And what a lovely picture they all made that morning, with their sleepy, joyful smiles and messy bed hair covered by floppy hats.

It was the Christmas gathering Helen had been dreaming of.

"Papa, read!" Ella, Tyler's little girl, came running up to Kevin, who sat beside Helen, his thick Bible a weight in her small pudgy hands.

Kevin set aside his mug of black decaf coffee, took the Bible from Ella with one hand, and pulled her onto his lap with the opposite arm. "It is that time, isn't it?" He looked around the room, and without a cue, the children all left whatever they were doing and gathered around Kevin and Helen, sitting on the floor.

After turning to the book of Luke, Kevin cleared his throat and then bowed his head. "Lord, bless the reading of Your Word. Let us hear Your story and be amazed all over again by Your great love. Amen."

Amens echoed in the room.

With his finger on the page, Kevin began to read. "Luke 2, the birth of Jesus. In those days . . ."

Helen listened to his deep, resonant voice and savored this moment. Like Mary did after the birth of her holy son, Helen treasured these things in her heart. From two broken and desperately lost people who had married more to cover up a pregnancy than to honor God, He had worked this: a room full of people she cherished. A family grown in faith.

They were a miracle. She was sitting in the middle of a forty-year-long miracle. And the best part?

God wasn't done yet.

Helen was certain of it—because there they were, still living. And after that? They would have a whole eternity to celebrate all that God had done.

Glory to God in the highest!

Glory. Glory! Glory indeed!

Kevin finished reading at verse 20, and as he reached for her, she took his hand.

Ella turned her cherub face upward and smiled. "Presents?"

Laughing, Kevin nodded. "Presents!"

All chaos broke loose. Soon paper and bags were everywhere. The room filled with all the unnecessary stuff that came with an American Christmas, but also with laughter and friendly banter.

Connor and Reid had given Lily and Kellen each a card that had caused a moment of mystery. Neither child read the contents aloud, but they exchanged a meaningful look, and then both moved to hug Connor. From her spot to the side of that group, Helen could hear Lily whisper, "Yes!" Kellen didn't say anything, but he did fist bump Reid.

Anticipation, and still a niggling of worry, threaded through Helen, but nothing followed. The family simply continued unwrapping Christmas. Somewhere in the midst of the madness, Brandon and Megan managed to slip an envelope into Helen's hands.

What she found inside made her laugh heartily. She had no idea that any of the boys had known the story of how she'd told Kevin about Brayden . . . but obviously they did.

The card inside the envelope held an ultrasound image and a note that read *I hear you're the best, so I can't wait to meet you, Grandma and Grandpa!*

Oh goodness! She had miscalculated those weeks ago when she was numbering the grands. Fifteen scurrying around now, yes. However, it was not *one* on the way, but with Brayden and Audrey's, Tyler and Becca's, and Brandon and Megan's as well, there were *three*!

They would have eighteen grandchildren!

Kevin had draped his arm around her and laughed along with her as they read the announcement. When Helen turned to search his eyes, she expected to find pure excitement there. And she did. But also an emotion she could only describe as humility.

Ah, this man. He did feel deeply. Helen covered his cheek with one palm and leaned in to kiss him. "It's so much more than we ever dreamed, isn't it?"

He shut his eyes for a breath and then nodded. "Exceedingly abundantly more than I could ever ask or imagine."

The wonderful noise of Christmas continued around them, but for that moment, it was only Helen and Kevin, their hearts lifted together in adoration of the God who could and had and would continue to be *more.*

Kevin dozed in his leather recliner, his belly full of moist turkey, cranberry salad, and homemade rolls. His heart, if it were possible, was fuller. This season had been *full.* And he thanked God he'd been allowed more time on the earth so he could experience it.

This life was such a gift.

Behind closed eyes, Kevin replayed the tender moments only shared between Helen and himself last night. Alone in their room, the house at last quiet, he had tugged her into his arms, and they began moving to the music of their hearts. Time after time he'd tasted the sweetness of her kisses and savored the whispered promise of *soon*.

Soon. He'd be fully recovered. Soon, they'd have the house to themselves again.

But for now, that Christmas day, he would wait. Because this joy was a delight as well. This family God had poured into his heart. This life of noise and chaos. This blessing beyond measure. It was all wonderful, and until his final breath, he would savor every bit of it.

"Hey, Dad!" Brayden called from the front door.

Kevin opened his eyes, finding that the room was empty. He looked at the son who had called him out of semi-sleep.

Brayden waved him out. "You're not going to want to miss this."

Kevin followed, grabbing a coat before he stepped onto the front deck. There he found Helen and most of the adult children, as well as a few of the grands.

"What are we doing?"

"Spying." Helen looked up at him with sheer delight and then pointed toward the road. Their elevated vantage point provided a peek between evergreens on the road to the left of the end of the drive, and in that frame stood a couple.

"Helen."

"Hush, you'll ruin it."

"I'm sure Connor wouldn't—"

"He told Brayden." Helen spun to cover Kevin's lips with her fingertips and then just as quickly pivoted back to watch.

Just in time too. Taking both of Jade's hands, Connor went down on one knee and looked up. There was a beat. Two. Three . . .

And then Jade was covering her mouth and nodding, and Connor was on his feet sweeping her up into his arms.

"I think she said yes!" Lily clapped her hands.

Audrey beamed at the girl she would soon claim as a niece. "Is that what the cards were about this morning?"

Sheer joy stretched Lily's smile wide as she nodded, and then a sudden slip of tears trickled next to her nose. "He asked us if we would take him and Reid. If we could be a family." She elbowed Kellen, who was standing next to her. "It was so sweet, right?"

"Mushy stuff." Kellen rolled his eyes. But he didn't quite suppress the grin playing at his lips.

Lily gave him a playful push. "Maybe you should pay attention. Someday you might need to know how to be sweet."

"Not anytime soon."

The group laughed, and Kevin looked back at the scene they'd been spying on. Connor now had Jade's hand in his as they resumed their walk back to the house. Even from that distance, Kevin could see his son's happiness.

And he was glad. So terribly, wonderfully glad.

What a Christmas this had been.

CHAPTER NINETEEN

(in which there is an ending . . . and a new beginning)

B reakfast was nearly over, which meant this season was nearly done. The boys had already packed up their families' things and loaded them in vehicles.

It was time to say goodbye for now. Jackson and Kenzie would see Brayden and Audrey to the airport. Matt, Tyler, and Connor would point their cars west and head over the pass toward their homes. Brandon and Megan would stay a few more days to help Tyler on a project, and then they would go north.

Only Jacob and Kate and their kids would be around nearby, as they'd moved back to Sugar Pine.

Kevin grappled with a mild sense of letdown, and he knew Helen was doing so as well. She had so looked forward to this gathering. And it had been wonderful.

But they had things to look forward to still. Just the two of them. After all, they were still due that second honeymoon. And beyond that, he had some new ideas brewing. Hand-hewn sturdy furniture, just like Tyler had implied. Jacob had already promised to get a website up and going for Kevin, and he was as excited about this idea as Tyler had been.

And also, there was this business of boondocking. Jacob and Kate highly recommended it. A few months over the summer perhaps. It was time to try something new.

And there was always the simple business of living. Waking up every day and choosing gratitude. Finding new ways of making Helen smile. And hearing all of the things from his sons when they called.

Hey, Dad, they'd start with, and every time his heart squeezed with a little bit of awe. *He* got to be their dad. And they loved him.

He knew all too well things could have been so very different. But for the mercy and grace of God.

That was exactly the legacy he wanted his children to leave with. To carry forward. They would go into their lives and take with them the enduring grace of God that had been pressed into him. A grace that had reshaped him, changed the direction he'd been going.

A grace that would carry them on, even beyond the span of Kevin's natural life.

He could not hope for a greater blessing than that.

"Boys, will you gather your families around one last time before you all head out?"

To a son, they nodded, then did exactly as asked. Within minutes the group was a large huddle. A beautiful testimony of love right there in the Murphy living room.

Kevin opened the Bible he'd taken up while the children had gathered and found Numbers 6. "These past weeks I've been reminded of the journey your mother and I have been on. I've spent a lot of time thinking back over my life and have been astonished time and again at the grace God has poured out on me. So before we go our separate ways, I want to send you out with a blessing."

He looked down at the text. "The Lord bless you and keep you. The Lord make his face shine on you and be gracious to you. The Lord turn his face toward you and give you peace."

He closed the book and looked at his sons, making eye contact with each. "I was handed a legacy of addiction and shame, but that is not the heritage

I give to you. My children, live as people blessed by God, redeemed, and called to holy lives. Walk in the freedom of Christ, who has set you free. Love as Christ has loved the church. Lead your families as humble servants.

"And now, as Paul wrote to the Ephesians, 'to him who is able to do immeasurably more than all we ask or imagine, according to his power that is at work within us, to him be glory.'"

"Let your lives be worship, my family, as you go out from here in peace."

And there was a corporate *amen*. Let it be so.

THE END.

My friends, it's with a few tears that I meet you at the end our Murphy Brothers stories! I so hope these journeys have meaning for you—that they have left with a longing to seek God, to worship Him, and to trust him, no matter what season you may be in.

Thank you sincerely for trusting me with your time! Would you do me the honor of posting a review so that others may know what you thought? I would appreciate it!

Now, I leave you with Daddy Murph's blessing:

Let your lives be worship, my friends, as you go out from here in peace.

www.ingramcontent.com/pod-product-compliance
Lightning Source LLC
Chambersburg PA
CBHW031913190626
46814CB00003BA/1266